A Certain Magical Index 16

KAZUMA KAMACHI

ILLUSTRATION BY
KIYOTAKA HAIMURA

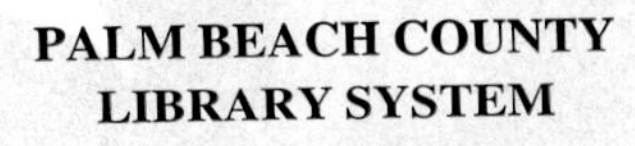

"Wh-what?! What the heck are you doing here?!"
Academy City Tokiwadai Middle School Level Five
Mikoto Misaka

"…You have to be quiet in the bath!"
Nun managing the Index of Prohibited Books **Index**

"…Acqua of the Back is coming. I'm sure of it."
Vicar pope of the Amakusa-Style Crossist Church **Saiji Tatemiya**

"Oh no, you mustn't get up!!"
Amakusa-Style Crossist Church follower **Itsuwa**
"Blah…Wait, what day is it?
I-I'm still okay on attendance, right?!"
Academy City High School student **Touma Kamijou**

"...I am both a saint *and* of God's Right Seat!!"
Member of God's Right Seat and a saint within the Roman Orthodox Church
Acqua of the Back

contents

VOLUME 16

KAZUMA KAMACHI
ILLUSTRATION BY: KIYOTAKA HAIMURA

NEW YORK

A CERTAIN MAGICAL INDEX, Volume 16
KAZUMA KAMACHI

Translation by Andrew Prowse
Cover art by Kiyotaka Haimura

First published in Japan in 2008 by KADOKAWA CORPORATION, Tokyo.
English translation rights arranged with KADOKAWA CORPORATION, Tokyo,
through Tuttle-Mori Agency, Inc., Tokyo.

Yen On
1290 Avenue of the Americas
New York, NY 10104

Visit us at yenpress.com
facebook.com/yenpress
twitter.com/yenpress
yenpress.tumblr.com
instagram.com/yenpress

First Yen On Edition: August 2018

Yen On is an imprint of Yen Press, LLC.
The Yen On name and logo are trademarks of Yen Press, LLC.

The publisher is not responsible for websites (or their content) that are not owned by the publisher.

Library of Congress Cataloging-in-Publication Data

Names: Kamachi, Kazuma, author. | Haimura, Kiyotaka, 1973– illustrator. | Prowse, Andrew (Andrew R.), translator. | Hinton, Yoshito, translator.
Title: A certain magical index / Kazuma Kamachi ; illustration by Kiyotaka Haimura.
Other titles: To aru majyutsu no index. (Light novel). English
Description: First Yen On edition. | New York : Yen On, 2014–
Identifiers: LCCN 2014031047 (print) | ISBN 9780316339124 (v. 1 : pbk.) | ISBN 9780316259422 (v. 2 : pbk.) | ISBN 9780316340540 (v. 3 : pbk.) | ISBN 9780316340564 (v. 4 : pbk.) | ISBN 9780316340595 (v. 5 : pbk.) | ISBN 9780316340601 (v. 6 : pbk.) | ISBN 9780316272230 (v. 7 : pbk.) | ISBN 9780316359924 (v. 8 : pbk.) | ISBN 9780316359962 (v. 9 : pbk.) | ISBN 9780316359986 (v. 10 : pbk.) | ISBN 9780316360005 (v. 11 : pbk.) | ISBN 9780316360029 (v. 12 : pbk.) | ISBN 9780316442671 (v. 13 : pbk.) | ISBN 9780316442701 (v. 14 : pbk.) | ISBN 9780316442725 (v. 15 : pbk.) | ISBN 9780316442749 (v. 16 : pbk.)
Subjects: | CYAC: Magic—Fiction. | Ability—Fiction. | Nuns—Fiction. | Japan—Fiction. | Science fiction. | BISAC: FICTION / Fantasy / General. | FICTION / Science Fiction / Adventure.
Classification: LCC PZ7.1.K215 Ce 2014 | DDC [Fic]—dc23
LC record available at https://lccn.loc.gov/2014031047

ISBNs: 978-0-316-44274-9 (paperback)
978-0-316-44275-6 (ebook)

1 3 5 7 9 10 8 6 4 2

LSC-C

Printed in the United States of America

PROLOGUE

A Leader's Position

Stage_in_Roma.

The Roman Orthodox pope had a certain vivid memory.

It was of a time when he had traveled to London for a meeting with the English Puritan Church.

One of the three major denominations of Catholicism, the English Church had a leader who was a woman of unknown age named Laura Stuart. To be sure, she had real ability—enough to tie the huge organization together. After all, she was incredibly skilled with words, easily concealing her own intentions and feelings, and by the time anyone caught on to the hidden purport and direction of whatever the matter of debate was, they'd already agreed with her. Let up for one moment, and who knew what sort of contracts she'd get you to sign. It got so bad that the three Roman Orthodox amanuenses attending with him broke under pressure and had to be brought to a medical office.

But for the pope of Rome, that wasn't the most brightly shining part of the memory. No, that was reserved for what happened thirty minutes after the assembly.

The location was Lambeth Palace, near St. George's Cathedral. The luxury vehicle carrying the Roman pontiff was just passing by the archbishop of the English Puritan Church's official residence when they came to a stop at a traffic signal. When he opened his window, he heard voices from the palace.

"The septembral month has scant started, but thusly are we receiving Christmas cards in abundance..."

"It'll be too late once Christmas is upon us. Getting them so early in the year proves they're considering our own circumstances. After all, it's a very laborious task to read two hundred fifty thousand Christmas cards sent from all throughout England every winter."

"You speak as if it concerns you not, Kanzaki."

"I don't know what you mean. Anyway, we've decided on a schedule for December. Archbishop, you'll be visiting forty-three child-welfare and family-shelter facilities dressed as Santa Claus. Please understand that this is a part of your official duties."

"Indeed. In fact, I have already procured for my personage a nosebleed-knockout miniskirt-style Santa dress."

"???!!! Did you just nod confidently, mutter *indeed*, and then say something crazy?!"

"Well, if I were to tell you the truth—and I am oh, so embarrassed about this—I have made the gut-twisting decision to strip the varnish for the sake of our devoted Anglican believers."

"You mean you're literally going to strip for this, you pervert?!"

"What?! Do you mean to say so many seasons have passed that miniskirted Santas are now received coldly enough to be called perverts?!"

"No, well, I...The issue is completely different—it's your choice as Archbishop of the English Church to wear a miniskirt in the first place, clothing that exposes so much of your legs, and—"

"Hmm. What you mean is that a miniskirt Santa wouldn't, as they say, get the job done? I suppose I am not one of the original photogravures who thrive on fan-service shots, yes? And this is coming from Kaori Kanzaki, who would seriously and literally strip for the Japanese cause of *debt repayment* for that illusion-killing boy. As expected of a woman who fights on the front lines of skin exposure."

"Lay off, you freaking novice!!"

"?!"

"I've been trying to listen politely, but you've done nothing but run your mouth! If it wasn't for you putting that weird-ass spell collar on *her* and then using her to get a weird-ass place to owe you something, I wouldn't have needed to repay a debt in the first place and Tsuchimikado wouldn't be incessantly teasing me!!"

"K-Kanzaki? Hello, Kanzaki…? Um, well, you aren't articulating like you customarily do, and—"

"I don't think *you* have any right to insult people for the way they talk, shithead!!"

"?! I—I think you've just said something I can't let slip by… O-okay, it's time for me to woman up and scold you. Kanzaki!! How dare you even thinketh of calling the head of the English Church such foul things?!!"

"Shut your trap, you amateur…I've made up my mind. Ever since that perverted freak Tsuchimikado laughed his ass off at me at the beach house, I knew this idiot woman was the cause of everything. I knew that if this moron wasn't here, I wouldn't have to repay any debts! And so I decided I'd stop respecting the imbecile entirely!!"

"E-eeeeek!! Stiyl, *Stiyl*!!"

A slam and a bang came from the direction of Lambeth Palace, followed by joyous shrieks and the awfully jaunty sounds of things breaking.

The exchange, in terms of decorum, doubtlessly warranted a failing grade. In fact, considering their statuses and ranks, the conversation never should have happened in the first place. The fact that sorcerers were letting others hear them from the Lambeth Palace, that most secretive of sanctuaries, was itself another problem. The housewives with their children walking nearby were at first startled by the women's archaic speech. Still, after that, they giggled to themselves and walked away.

It was all incomprehensible.

But the only things he could see were smiles.

Before him was a world where age distinctions, power relations, and authority and dignity in one's faith weren't part of the picture. A world that was simply *equal*. The pope watched it idly, sitting in the backseat of his black luxury car surrounded by several guards.

She certainly didn't seem like the same woman who had so easily handled their world-changing assembly in St. George's Cathedral. But at the same time, she didn't seem to be straying too far from the Crossist teachings. The Father who watches over all believers said this: Love thy neighbor, all men are brothers, and all are equal before the Lord. Was that not exactly what was happening here?

Things got more difficult with every added layer, like age and position.

The higher wasn't *only* trying to act with equality toward the lower. The lower wasn't *just* trying not to anger the higher. Laura Stuart would fight anyone, insult them, carry on, and sometimes get a little teary-eyed. But in the very end, laughter was all that remained.

That was the Archbishop of Canterbury, leader of the English Puritan Church.

A decade ago, two decades ago…even from the first time he'd ever visited the land of England, he was sure the woman, whose age was indiscernible, had always been smiling like this.

Smiling amid everyone else—smiling along with them.

As he wallowed in nostalgia, the pope of Rome walked the streets of Italy's capital city.

He had just come to the Vatican to give a short speech at the Church of Sant'Agostino, and now he was on his way back. It was about a kilometer and a half to get there. Whenever the pope was doing something in Rome, he preferred to go there on foot rather than use a courtesy car—partly because it was simply healthier, partly because he enjoyed breathing the air in Rome, and partly because he wanted to make contact with as many of the everyday people as possible.

In fact, even now, there was a tourist who froze in place and forgot to even take out his camera and an older woman praying deeply from a window.

However…

"…One cannot call this situation desirable," whispered the male secretary next to him, so that only he could hear. Although the man held the title of "secretary," he was actually a martial protection officer. Changing his title had given him the right to stay by the pontiff's side even in places armed individuals weren't allowed to enter.

He went on: "I still believe it's too risky to be walking around. We have several guards in the vicinity right now, but it's not perfect, I'm afraid. We should assemble a convoy of vehicles with magical protection to move around."

"I know that."

"If you believe all Crossists being equal is important in this case, then there are other efficient methods we could also adopt. We can bump your favorability by visiting more child-welfare and family-shelter facilities and medical facilities to—"

"I said, I know that," repeated the pope, this time more strongly, his mood now ruined.

The secretary fell quiet.

The pope heaved a sigh. He always sought equality, but it didn't seem to be working. The pedestrians and tourists who looked at him simply gave him stares of surprise and respect. They didn't feel at all as though they were part of his "circle," as had been the case with Laura Stuart previously.

Then a filthy ball rolled out from a tight alleyway. It was about thirty centimeters across. A cheap-looking toy for children, made of a shiny material that looked like vinyl or rubber.

Without a second thought, the pope bent to pick up the ball, but his secretary intervened with his hand. When the pope stopped, a child burst out of the alleyway after it. She must have been a street child; they were rare in this area. She was about ten years old, and her clothes were even dirtier than the earth-covered toy.

The pope swatted his secretary's hand out of the way and went to pick up the ball again.

But before he could, a sharp voice cut him off. "Stop."

He looked to see that it was the girl.

"I might get in big trouble if I get your fancy clothes dirty," she said.

The coldness in her voice made the pope freeze in place as though struck by lightning. Meanwhile, the girl grabbed the ball, slowly backed away from him with wary caution as though he were a ruffian, then fled back into the narrow alley whence she came.

"..."

He could do nothing but stand in a stupor.

Love thy neighbor. All men are brothers. All are equal before the Lord.

As those words came to mind, he clenched his teeth. "This is a problem...," he said abruptly.

The secretary next to him nodded. "Yes. That was quite rude behavior toward the Bishop of Rome, single leader of two billion believers strong. We must not allow such things. And in Italy, the very home of our faith, of all places...I'm sure you would appreciate it if those calling themselves believers kept at least a minimum of good character."

"..." The pope sighed at the secretary. The man didn't understand a single thing.

How long had it been like this?

At this point, the only thing he could feel was a chill, brought on by this alien sense of isolation.

CHAPTER 1

Course from Peace to Ruination

Battle_of_Collapse.

1

Certain circumstances dictated that fourth period dragged on for an abnormally long time today.

By the time everyone in class, including perfectly ordinary high school student Touma Kamijou, ran to the school store and cafeteria, their window of opportunity was perfectly shut. They were late for everything: The bread at the store was wiped out, and the cafeteria seats were all taken, the latter with no signs of improving before lunch break was over. To put the nail in the coffin, the food-ticket vending machine was blinking all its lined-up lights on and off, emptier than a cigarette machine at midnight.

It was rotten luck, and it was all because of a tangent during class, wherein Touma Kamijou had asked his history teacher this question: "Huh. Then what would Japan be like now, if Nobunaga Oda had made a Nobunaga Shogunate, instead of Tokugawa?"

Kamijou, feeling responsible, went to the faculty room to make a direct appeal. As Miss Komoe munched on her 580-yen healthy soba set meal served on a bamboo basket dish, he requested, "If you can, please open the Home Ec room! I'll open up a new place—Restaurant Kamijou!! Featuring spectacular creations using leftover cold rice, grated cheese, and ketchup!"

However, his teacher didn't respond to his desperate plea with anything more than a pained smile. Plus, thanks to his math teacher Suama Oyafune digging ravenously into her gorgeous sea urchin- and salmon-topped rice bowl, as well as his gym teacher Aiho Yomikawa having already put away several steamed meat buns that didn't look very much like a lunch, the faculty room was filled with nothing but annoyingly delicious scents. The atmosphere in the room had forced Kamijou to flee before he lost control.

"Th-the only road left is the drink machine…but will it last us all through afternoon classes?"

Motoharu Tsuchimikado and Blue Hair joined Kamijou to lament the food crisis, followed by Aisa Himegami (who had forgotten to make her own lunch for once), Seiri Fukiyose (who was fresh out of mail-order health foods), the rest of the cafeteria group, and the school store group. Their coed hoard numbered twenty-one in all.

And as the Packed Lunch Alliance enjoyed a veritable feast with their incredibly tasty-looking hamburgers and pork dumplings, the members of the Starving Federation finally made their decision.

"We have to bust out and go to the convenience store!!"

Who could have shouted that?

The next thing they knew, the boys and girls of the cafeteria and school store groups, the Starving Federation, had formed a circle and begun a war council.

Seiri Fukiyose had to be the one to show her strength at a time like this. "If all of us leave school at once, the teachers will find out. We should narrow our team down to three or four people, have everyone give them their money, and have them buy us food. It would be more efficient!!"

"What should the rest of us do?" asked Himegami, tilting her head.

Kamijou raised his hand. "Gather information, create diversions, and stick to other backup stuff, right? We have to make sure the teachers don't find out about this. I need everyone's help. Keep your cell phones on. We need the latest intel—or else this will result in failure."

"Great. Now we need to figure out where to escape from, nya!" Tsuchimikado flipped over a piece of paper he didn't need anymore and sketched a detailed map of the school on it. "Here are all the alarms that detect suspicious people," he said. "The infrared sensors are active only at night, so we don't need to worry about them... Considering where the faculty room is, they'll spot us right away if we leave from the main entrance, since they can see the whole schoolyard from their window, nya. We'll have to use the back door. But that's where the man from the school store goes in and out. If we run into him, we'll have a really rough time, nya."

"I see...," said Fukiyose. "We'll have to time our exit carefully, then. All right, I'll give everyone their roles now!!"

At her instructions, the twenty-one rebels split into several groups. She, Kamijou, Tsuchimikado, and Blue Hair would be the four in the team actually making the escape. Apparently, she had an opinion of them as highly alert based on the shenanigans they always encountered.

"But Kamijou's got rotten luck. Should we really let him get our lunch?"

"We'll be fine. He has a very important role—the decoy."

Kamijou raised his fist to quiet the classmates whispering about him.

Still in the huddle, everyone took out their cell phones, set them on transceiver mode so they could connect to multiple lines at once, and then made sure their digital clocks were precise down to the second.

"Time to go. Mission—start!!"

Clap-clap! Fukiyose put her hands together, and then the cafeteria and school store group split off like scattering spiders.

Kamijou, Blue Hair, Tsuchimikado, and Fukiyose, while in a hurry, purposely walked through the hall slowly enough to look like they were in no rush. That way, nobody would stop them for running in the halls.

"This mission will be a race against time," said Fukiyose, trading smiles with several teachers along the way as they speed walked. "Convenience stores make the most profits during lunchtime. Even if we manage to get outside, this will all be for nothing if the lunches are gone from the shelves!!"

They didn't go to the shoe cupboards. If anyone spotted them changing out of their slippers and loafers, they'd know they were trying to leave. And if their shoes were absent and they weren't in the schoolyard...that would be relatively fatal.

Instead, they had a separate group grab their gym shoes. After trading their slippers for those, they went to the "path to the outside" connecting the school building to the gymnasium, put on their gym shoes, then broke out. They ran behind the school building before anyone could nab them.

The metal fence was in sight. Nobody was around. The possible complication—the man from the school store—was nowhere to be seen.

"Great! Let's keep going right out of here!!"

Kamijou enthusiastically tried to climb over the fence.

That was when it happened.

Beep! Beep! The shrill sound of claxons.

He turned around and saw the gorilla-like Mr. Saigo there, apparently returning from a family restaurant where he'd eaten lunch.

Their educational guidance counselor was riding in a family-use four-door car, but they'd discriminated against gorillas when they made it, because it looked as cramped as a public phone booth for him.

"No!!" cried Fukiyose. "We should have considered the possibility that a teacher could be using the back entrance to get to their car!!"

She regretted her oversight, but Kamijou felt differently.

He simply shouted what was on his mind.

"What a coward!! Eating out *now* of all times?! That muscle-monster counselor was on his own enjoying a relaxed atmosphere in a restaurant while we were fighting tooth and nail in a cafeteria that isn't big enough?!"

"K-Kammy, idiot, don't yell at him! If we get caught here, what will become of everyone's lunch?!"

Blue Hair's voice snapped Kamijou out of his indignance.

The gorilla-like teacher, Mr. Saigo, got out of the car and started stampeding straight for them. To get away, Kamijou went over the metal fence and fled. Fukiyose, sensing that sticking together was disadvantageous, immediately started down a different escape route. Just as Tsuchimikado was about to be caught, he kicked Blue Hair off the fence, then set off a flare used for evading missiles.

Kamijou and Tsuchimikado wouldn't let his noble sacrifice be in vain, so they ran full speed down the road outside school.

As Tsuchimikado darted away, he looked over his shoulder—and had a fright.

"That damn gorilla!" he shouted. "He's tied Blue Hair down, and now he's coming after us!!"

"Seriously?! Tsuchimikado, let's split up for now! We can't afford to get wiped out here!!"

They nodded to each other, then went their separate ways at an intersection to maximize their chances of survival.

2

Itsuwa, a girl belonging to the Amakusa-Style Crossist Church, was near Kamijou's high school.

She was wearing a pink tank top over a fluffy, sheeplike sweater, and below those, dark pants...but the pants had spiraling pieces cut out of them, with a clear vinyl material holding it all together so it wouldn't flip upward—a brand-new Academy City design made to show a bold amount of leg. This was a rare city, 80 percent of its citizens being students, and in cities, even this one, she chose her clothes very carefully, in order to blend in with people. For a business neighborhood, she'd wear a suit, and for a shopping mall, a miniskirt. This went for both Itsuwa and the rest of Amakusa.

She had a reason for being in Academy City.

Two days prior, the leaders of the English Puritan Church and Academy City each received a copy of the same letter. The sender was a member of God's Right Seat, a top-secret Roman Orthodox group, named Acqua of the Back. It contained the following: *I go now to obliterate Touma Kamijou. If you wish to stop me, do so with all your might*—a letter of challenge.

It could have been a fake, of course. However, the letter sent to the English Church had a certain item attached to it, unlike the one sent to Academy City, that supplied trustworthiness.

The remains of Terra of the Left.

In addition to being gently wrapped in the finest-quality velvet, they were packed in a box of faintly scented paulownia wood. It was decorated extravagantly, almost like a jewel box. Was it a show of scorn toward his enemies or a display of respect?

Because she'd directly fought with Terra, Itsuwa had been called to St. George's Cathedral to verify the remains…and that was where the confusion had started.

There were two reasons. The first was that Terra should have been incinerated in Avignon by an Academy City weapon—but the remains clearly showed his body severed at the waist.

The second was that if Terra *had* withstood the Academy City weapon—and Acqua of the Back had executed him so easily—what did that say about *his* strength?

A single blow. That was all they could say, looking at the wound.

Having battled Terra of the Left personally, Itsuwa knew how strong he was. He had put her and the others through terrible suffering. He'd even broken through the front of a large military unit deployed by Academy City. And then, his entire body was ripped apart—a gruesome end if there ever was one.

There was another question.

God's Right Seat hadn't been using roundabout tactics before now. Why had they sent an old-fashioned letter of challenge? Why had Acqua personally killed Terra of the Left and used him as a foundation for his challenge?

Acqua of the Back's extremely straightforward approach put the Church and Academy City off in several ways. They knew it was probably a trap, but they couldn't discern the true intentions behind it. Still, he'd said he was coming after Touma Kamijou, so he must have decided defeating him here was the best option. That, in turn, led to the English Church dispatching the Amakusa-Style Crossist Church here.

Normally, any group actions by sorcerers were forbidden in Academy City. The act was seen as divisive between the magic side and the science side.

But this time, due to an exception, they'd broken the agreement. Itsuwa didn't know the details, but the English Church's archbishop had most likely had a word with Academy City leaders. Amakusa was a small, independent group under the English Church's umbrella; maybe they'd decided it was the right time to cut off the lizard's tail, as it were, now that things were getting bad. Or they could have also decided on people who were familiar with the lay of the land, as Amakusa had originally been active in Japan. Whatever the case, Itsuwa, who was not supposed to be here, was currently in Academy City.

Part of the reason was that the world had begun forming sides: Academy City and the English Puritan Church on one side and the Roman Orthodox and Russian Catholic Churches on the other. A larger reason was that Acqua of the Back was a potent bomb. They wouldn't be able to defeat him without breaking the rules.

On the other hand, the bigger threat wasn't the global chaos this science-sorcery divide would cause. It was Acqua of the Back's lone attack run, and both the city and the English Church had accepted that. They knew how strong the man was, and they treated him with appropriate importance.

"..."

That was why they'd decided to have Itsuwa take part in the conflict as Kamijou's bodyguard.

At the same time, though she was smart and sensible and knew she had to contact him as soon as possible, she wasn't about to rush into his school during classes. Right now, her plan was to wait in a spot easily visible from his classroom, and then once school let out for the day, she'd get this show on the road.

...I have to do my best, she thought, making a small fist, secretly enthusiastic.

During the Document C incident, her lack of skill had prevented her from protecting Kamijou to the end. This time, she would approach this like a professional sorcerer, not letting anyone lay a finger on the civilian.

She reaffirmed her grip on the bag over her shoulder and felt the weight of the disassembled Friulian spear inside it. *They're talking about how he's already taken down two of God's Right Seat—Vento of the Front and Terra of the Left. But there must be something I can do. That's why I have to do my best.*

Just then, a familiar person shot past Itsuwa.

It was the boy himself—Touma Kamijou.

"Huh?"

Why? wondered Itsuwa, checking the time. School definitely hadn't let out yet. Plus, the look on his face as he ran down the street was odd. It was almost like somebody was chasing him.

Maybe something had happened. A hint of tension flared through her eyes.

Then she saw some kind of big, gorilla-looking man dash past her in pursuit.

He had the face of one of those blocky-looking bad guys who appeared a lot in individualistic western video games.

There was no way that gorilla was a regular person. Even Touma Kamijou, a hardened war veteran, had a face full of terror. She could see the words written on his face: *He'll rip me apart!*

Eventually, she made her decision. According to the report from September 30, Acqua of the Back was male.

He didn't waste any time getting here!! she thought, swiftly assembling her spear and charging off toward the game-like villain.

3

Mr. Saigo, the educational guidance instructor, ended up going home early due to health issues.

"...Blah."

After school, Kamijou, who had managed to complete the grand lunchtime mission, heaved a sigh as he changed his indoor slippers for his outdoor basketball shoes before leaving the school gate. Itsuwa was standing around, her face still pale.

For some reason, Itsuwa (complete with her lance) had shown up out of the blue during the lunch break and, with the look of a monster, had delivered a fierce tackle to his educational guidance instructor.

It seemed she had jumped the gun: "That...wasn't Acqua of the Back? What? A schoolteacher?!" she'd said in a fluster. "H-he has a face like that and he's a *teacher*?!"

It looked like she really needed to talk about why she was here, but in order to smooth things over with the gorilla teacher, whose eyes were spinning, she had picked the man up and moved him swiftly to a hospital.

Which brought things to now.

"Could...Could I be any more useless...?"

When she came back from the hospital, her face had been dark and depressed.

For Kamijou, it would have all been over if the gorilla had caught him. Kamijou knew he would have slammed him to the asphalt with an ultra-powerful ancient martial art throw, then comboed that into sweaty groundwork techniques. In terms of her usefulness, he would have said 100 percent yes, she'd been very useful. But it didn't seem like that was the reason she was so blue.

As for hurting a regular person... Well, that gorilla is legendary for stopping a chunk of bedrock in a "watch for falling rocks" zone with his bare hands. I'm really, really not sure whether to call him a regular person.

Whatever the case, Kamijou decided to ask Itsuwa, a resident of the magic side, why she was in Academy City, home base of the science side.

With much trepidation, she replied, "Do you remember the name Acqua of the Back?"

Kamijou's brows knitted in suspicion. "One of God's Right Seat, right? I met him on September thirtieth."

Yes—after he'd defeated Vento of the Front in Academy City, Acqua of the Back had stepped in to intervene. He was both a member of God's Right Seat and someone with the qualities of a saint. Kamijou couldn't fathom his actual battle strength, but he at least knew he was way above all the enemies he'd fought until now.

Not particularly heading anywhere, they ended up walking toward the shopping district. Kamijou asked, "Anyway, why do you ask about Acqua? He's not starting shady business in some city in another country, is he?"

"N-no, it's not that..." Itsuwa was having a lot of trouble getting the words out. She went over it in her mind a few times, then finally said, "We think Acqua of the Back is after you."

"What?"

"Well, both the English Puritan Church and Academy City got a threatening letter from Acqua of the Back. He said he would ob—attack you in a few days, and to get ready." She cut herself off midword, worried, like a parent trying to explain something to their child while softening some of the more upsetting parts.

Kamijou was dubious. He was an average high school student. He didn't quite grasp the severity of God's Right Seat and Acqua of the Back being after his life.

"God's Right Seat, huh...?" He thought for a moment. "From what Vento of the Front said, they were forcing the pope to make documents just so they could come and kill me, or attack Academy City, or whatever. It seems like a stupidly high cost just to get one high school kid. I wonder why they're doing it again."

"Huh?! No, no, no, no!! It's because you've been helping so many people, and stopping the Roman Orthodox Church's shadow groups' schemes, and doing all sorts of other things, and I guess what I'm trying to say is that whether or not you're in high school doesn't have anything to do with it..."

He didn't really know why Itsuwa was getting so flustered and crying out. He decided to chalk it up to Amakusa's favoritism of him. It tickled Kamijou to be flattered like that, but he was genuinely nothing more than a simple high schooler. Even if they praised him, nothing would come of it.

"Anyway, we had 'the Front' and 'the Left' before, so...it's Acqua 'of the Back' this time, huh?"

"The British Library is investigating him right now, but they haven't gotten anything relevant nor anything on the other God's Right Seat members."

"Well, they are secret members of a covert organization after all."

"We can't find any details about his power as a member of God's Right Seat, but he seems to have the powers of a saint, too. We might have asked the Priestess to help, but..."

The "Priestess" was Kaori Kanzaki. She was another of the less than twenty saints in the world. Her feats included once fighting against an actual angel and surviving.

Her assistance would be reassuring, but for various reasons, there was a valley between her and Amakusa. On top of that, based on what people like Stiyl had told him, the immense power saints had didn't necessarily let them move around at will.

"...But that isn't to say we don't have a plan," said Itsuwa, meaning to wipe away the young man's unease. "God's Right Seat is extremely strong on the magic side, and there's honestly no guarantee we could hope to stand up to them even in an advantageous battle. But Vento of the Front, Terra of the Left...We successfully drove them both off, and why is that?"

"Hmm."

"I haven't done a detailed analysis, so I can't say this is confirmed information, but there is one thing linking them: They faced large-scale interference from the science side. The powered suits and supersonic bombers forced Terra of the Left to change his plans, and as for Vento of the Front...um...Something about people seeing an angel?"

She might be on to something. The thing that shook God's Right Seat, one of the strongest groups on the magic side, was always an irregular counterattack from the science side. That meant maybe the key to victory was not to fight them on a stage they had perfect supremacy on but to drag them to the disadvantageous science side and make them fight there.

"That would mean," he said, "there's something really important about them fighting in Academy City, since it's full of science."

"I...I don't think that's the only thing, but..."

"?"

Kamijou tilted his head in confusion as Itsuwa stammered, but she waved her hands to pass it off. "A-anyway! If Acqua attacks, I'll be sure to protect you!" she announced enthusiastically. "We're under orders from the English Church to guard you both openly and from the shadows, so please don't worry!!"

There was one small thing he couldn't let slide. He figured he might have misheard her, so he asked again, just to be sure. "And why are you here, Itsuwa?"

"I'm here to guard you, of course," she said, clenching a small fist in excitement.

Kamijou blinked. He decided to ask again. "And why are you here, Itsuwa?"

"I told you, I'm here to guard you. Which means I'll be staying with you."

4

From behind cover, Saiji Tatemiya, vicar pope of the Amakusa-Style Crossist Church, lowered his binoculars.

They were right next to a small movie theater. Nearby was a narrow byway with a lottery vendor set up at its entrance that blocked the view. It was a queer place, the sort that was near large numbers of people but hard to see.

He narrowed his eyes with a sour expression, binoculars in one hand. Quietly, he said, "What a bore."

The large man next to him, Ushibuka, who was pretending to read a magazine, nodded. "Come on, Itsuwa...," he murmured. "She's acting like this is just business. Not going in for the attack at all."

"You've got that right. We finally gave her the chance to engage Touma Kamijou at point-blank range, and not only is she refusing to appeal herself to him—she doesn't even know her own weapons."

"What do you mean by weapons?" asked a short boy named Kouyagi as he munched on some popcorn.

Tatemiya fished around in the bag on the ground next to him. Then he brought out a flip-board—the kind quiz show contestants wrote answers on—and began squeaking and scribbling on it with a black marker.

He'd written down the right answer and theatrically whipped it around to show them. Then, *bam!!* His eyes popped open. "That's right—the 'Itsuwa secretly has giant tits' theory!!" he declared.

They all scampered up to him in a rush—not only Ushibuka and Kouyagi but the whole male crowd, including Isahaya, an older man, and Nomozaki, who was already married.

"D-do you have any proof for that theory, Vicar Pope?!"

"These better not be random predictions! Save them for the horse races, asshole!!"

The men began breathing raggedly. Tatemiya put his black marker to the flip-board again. "According to the results of the investigation from the Itsuwa Massage Stratagem that I executed earlier," he said, "her shoulder stiffness index is forty. But considering her physical strength and the amount of exercise she gets, even factoring in the total weight of her clothing, equipment, and possessions, her stiffness index should only be thirty-seven at most. It's odd!"

"You mean..." The group gulped.

Tatemiya nodded gravely, drew upon the deepest reserves of his strength, and declared in a loud voice, "Yes. This index differential of three proves my theory that Itsuwa secretly has huge tits!!"

Bum-bum!! With the stunning truth appended to the flip-board now in front of them, Ushibuka and Kouyagi fell to their knees. Isahaya, their elder, made an arm pump as if joyful at the growth of a grandchild. Meanwhile, Nomozaki, perhaps preferring them on the smaller side, drooped his shoulders in frustration.

Off to the side, Tsushima, a woman with fluffy golden locks standing a short distance away, sighed at the stupidity. "Quit the horseplay and focus on keeping track of the one we're guarding."

Tatemiya and the other men, their fun spoiled, gave Tsushima's body, tall yet light on cleavage, a thorough look from head to toe.

"Tsushima's an ambiguous one," said Kouyagi. "I don't think there's much demand for girls like her."

"What?!"

"Indeed," agreed Isahaya. "You'd think she'd at least have the good grace to be tall and big-breasted, or short with smaller ones. It's like the character designer didn't know what to do with her. What are we supposed to do?"

As Tsushima's mouth hung open in silence, Tatemiya pulled out another flip-board and wrote on it with his marker. "Tsk, tsk," he said. "The lot of you wouldn't understand this—my 'Tsushima has curvaceous legs' theory!!"

Before he could go any further explaining his strange ideas, Tsushima kicked him in the crotch to shut him up. The other men, not seeming very interested in her, left her alone and went back to Itsuwa.

"You think this is all right? It looks like Itsuwa's trying to continue her hand towel tactics."

"No, Itsuwa's too slow to mature," muttered Isahaya, clenching his teeth in frustration. "Nothing will happen like this..."

Tatemiya, oddly teary-eyed, wrested back control of the conversation. "You're right. If Itsuwa wants to use my 'extra-large oranges' theory to its fullest, she'll need to do more."

"E-extra-large oranges?!" cried Ushibuka in a fluster. "I thought they were apples at best!!"

Kouyagi looked dubious. "Vicar Pope, we're in the outfield. I don't think crying about it will solve the problem. Itsuwa's lack of maturity is tried and true at this point."

"Heh. That's why I brought a secret plan along." Tatemiya smirked and took something out of his bag of wonders.

"A soccer ball?"

"I propose what I'm calling the Grand Free Kick Strategy, carried out by yours truly—the sniper on the field, Saiji Tatemiya."

5

Mikoto Misaka's mind was hazy and murky.

It had been this way ever since she'd learned a certain thing about Touma Kamijou.

Thinking about it didn't solve it. Time passing didn't solve it. Her thoughts were going over it again and again, fruitlessly, like someone was making her solve a question that had no answer.

It couldn't possibly have been a lie.

The thing—it was his amnesia. That one word had shaken her heart.

But how long ago was it…?

When they'd signed up for the paired cell phone contract on November 30, he hadn't seemed strange. She couldn't see any changes in him during the Daihasei Festival, either. What about August 31? And back when he was involved with the Sisters and Accelerator?

"…" She couldn't get a grip on the problem. Now that she was thinking about it, he'd always seemed close to her. But there was a lot about him she couldn't actually figure out.

I know worrying about this isn't going to help…

How long had he been like this? How much of his memory had he lost? Did it affect his life? Did he ever see a doctor like he should have? Was there really no hope of curing him?

And—what parts of his memories had disappeared?

I guess I could talk about this with a mental-type esper I know, but...

There was one other Level Five at Tokiwadai Middle School besides Mikoto. She was number five and had the strongest mental-type ability in Academy City's history—Mental Out, as it was called. Reading memories, brainwashing personalities, telepathically talking to distant people, erasing feelings, amplifying willpower, reproducing thoughts, transplanting emotions...She had single-handedly mastered every mind-related phenomenon out there; she was a veritable Swiss Army knife of a Level Five.

"But I just don't like her...," Mikoto went on, speaking her thoughts aloud accidentally. It went to show how uncomfortable *she* made her.

After all, unlike Mikoto, who didn't belong to any specific groups, organizations, or factions, this girl had ascended to queenhood of the largest faction in the school. That in itself meant they wouldn't get along. If Mikoto asked her about this, it would undoubtedly place her in the girl's debt...and, at worst, she could always play a trick on that idiot's mind and lie that she cured it. The blunt fact was that she didn't trust her enough with his body.

Mikoto knew she shouldn't pursue that plan, so she drove the Level Five from her mind for the moment. *And I know this is that idiot's problem—not mine. But I can't just stop thinking about it. I'm not the kind of person who can have a rational attitude toward everything.*

Why hadn't he told her about it? Would it be better if she pretended not to notice? She couldn't give those questions, among other things, any more than a vexed clenching of her teeth. After all, Kamijou didn't seem to know Mikoto had realized any of this, and he seemed to want it that way. She could awkwardly question him about it and force him to talk, but...in this case, that could end up only hurting him.

What should she do? *Could* she do anything about this problem?

Graaahhh!! Crap. Why the heck am I even worrying over that idiot?! Now I'm all impatient and confused, and that's just making me more impatient. Maybe I should do a complete refresh and think about it from the beginning.

Still, if she could start thinking about something else just like that, she wouldn't be suffering now. She heaved a heavy sigh.

"…?" Suddenly, she caught sight of someone sneaking around near a small movie theater on a street corner.

The big man, his hair a glossy black like a stag beetle, placed a soccer ball on the asphalt. He took a few steps back to give himself some room, nodded to several others nearby, and then launched a full-force free kick.

Pom! The soccer ball flew far, rotating horizontally, its spin giving it a sharp curve. It was so strong that in an official game, it probably would have flown by the defense's wall and shot into the goal from the side.

Why were they doing this in the middle of the city? Mikoto, naturally, glanced at where the ball was headed.

And then she froze.

Ba-gam!! The ball struck Touma Kamijou in the side of the head.

And then the momentum sent his head flying into the cleavage of a nearby girl.

The force seemed to be so strong that Kamijou left his head buried in her chest, unconscious. The girl didn't seem to know what to do in response, and as her face reddened, she decided to rub the spot the ball hit with her palm. The act made it look like she was squeezing his head in, but that wasn't true, was it?

As Mikoto's mouth opened and closed in amazement, she heard a "Yahoo!" from somewhere. She looked over and saw the stag beetle who had done the abrupt free kick from the roadside and a group of young people cheering and giving one another high fives.

Snap-snap. She heard sparks flying.

Before she realized she was producing a high-voltage current, she exploded. "Here I am, worrying my butt off…Quit kicking that stupid ball around to try to get weird things to happen!!"

Spears of lightning went *zz-bam, zz-bam* from her bangs in succession. When the stag beetle's group saw, they scattered in all directions and disappeared in the blink of an eye. Like chameleons, they blended into the crowd, and although she looked, she couldn't find a single one of them.

"???" Mikoto tilted her head in confusion.

But just because she'd lost sight of her targets didn't mean her anger was quelled. After all, the source of everything, that spiky-haired boy, still had his face buried in that girl's chest. And then he started groaning in his sleep and clutching her breasts.

"That idiot…How long are you going to let those big clumps of motherhood coddle you?!" she shouted, dashing straight for Kamijou to deliver his punishment.

6

It had been a terrible day.

Touma Kamijou heaved a sigh.

A sudden free kick had hit him from the roadside; follow-up lightning attacks had struck him from Mikoto…Then she pinioned Itsuwa, who was starting to assemble her lance to do her bodyguard duty, and then he had to flee all over Academy City because for some reason Mikoto was angry about him being so close to Itsuwa. He'd run so far and gotten so much exercise that he knew he wouldn't have to worry at all about his metabolism.

And then, a new problem stood blocking his way.

Yes—this was where things got dicey.

"…Anyway, Touma, why is Itsuwa from Amakusa with you?"

The most dangerous checkpoint of the day.

The words Index had spoken as soon as he'd opened the door caused him to break out into a greasy sweat all over. She flashed her teeth, as if to say she was primed and ready to bite him at any time. Incredibly scary.

Incidentally, the calico cat always with her was circling Itsuwa, sniffing around, wondering who the new person was.

Kamijou wiped away some of the sweat on his brow. "W-well, you see," he started. "How should I explain this…?"

Itsuwa, standing next to him with a blank expression, said, "What he's trying to say is that God's Right Seat—"

"*Hi-yaaah*!!" Kamijou suddenly let out a cry and gave Itsuwa a karate chop to the neck. Her body jolted, and then he went around behind and put her in a headlock before hastily dragging her away from Index and beginning secret talks.

"(…Itsuwa, please!! Um, well, could I possibly get you to kindly keep this a secret from Index?!)" he whispered urgently.

"Wh-what?!"

"(…Acqua's only after me, so I think it would be best if he doesn't have to go after Index, too! Please don't say anything that will get her any closer to weird situations like this, okay?! Okay?!)"

"*Wawawawawawawawawawawawawawawawawawawa?!*"

"(…Itsuwa, are you listening to me?)"

"I-I'm listening!! I got all of that—yes, I did!!"

Itsuwa shook her head rapidly, her face for some reason bright red. *Am I hurting her?* he wondered. He put his arm around her shoulder and neck and grabbed her arm, but mysteriously enough, her expression turned somewhat unhappy.

And then…

"…"

Index, at some point, had gone completely stone-faced. She didn't even explode in a fuss. "Whatever," she muttered, turning back to the television again.

That made things very awkward. She was serious. This wasn't her calling him stupid over and over. He saw the kind of dark aura he noticed around his classmate Himegami sometimes. Why did it come to this? And why on earth was she so angry? After Kamijou shook back and forth, he eventually assumed a quiet groveling position, his head pointing at Index's back.

"…Well, I don't really understand, but would you mind biting me *before* you completely explode? If you let the power of your anger disperse little by little like this, Mr. Kamijou would get away without any bites to the skull, you know."

Despite Itsuwa's uncertain fidgeting at the two of them being so still, it was perhaps her sense of duty that made her stick to her role of guardian. Her gaze drifted from one spot to the next until her eyes met with the cat's as he finished smelling her.

"O-oh, that's right. I brought a gift for the cat," she said, not to calm the situation but to remove herself from the uncomfortable conversation, fishing around in her big bag.

What? thought Kamijou. *How did she know we had a cat at the Kamijou residence?*

No sooner had she removed a super-expensive-looking golden can with the words *Feast for a Cat: Three-Star Platinum Rank* on it than the cat froze with his hair on end. His eyes opened wide as his posture returned to normal. Itsuwa popped the lid off and offered it to him, but he seemed scared of it, as though saying, *I may be a cat, but are you sure you want to feed me something so bourgeois?!*

Then Kamijou, still in his highly rated groveling position, got a glimpse of a supermarket bag inside Itsuwa's tote.

"...Why do you have meat and vegetables in your bag, Itsuwa?" he asked. "Are they for an Amakusa-Style secret fish spell?"

"N-no, nothing like that," she said, waving her hands in front of her face. "Right now, I don't have any food restrictions like fasting. I just got some ingredients at a nearby supermarket in advance. I, well, I can make simple things. I may be a bodyguard, but I would balk at freeloading. You can leave the housework to me. I'll help with whatever I'm able to."

For a moment, Kamijou didn't understand what she'd just said. It took several blank seconds for him to finally realize the meaning of her commendable remark. This time, without a word, he moved his head around to look at Index.

"Wh-what, Touma?" she said. "Why does it feel like our positions just changed?"

"Look inside your heart for the answer. Who, exactly, has been leaving everything to poor Kamijou and refusing to help at all?"

"O-oh. Well, I'm sorry, but...Wait! You're just saying that to try and turn the tables on me—"

She was about to see through his scheme, but now that the flow had turned against her, it wouldn't change. Kamijou, indeed naturally, looked over toward his kitchen space. "Um, do you need me to tell you where the pots are?"

"Oh, yes, please."

Their exchange left the nun in white out of the picture, and the questions he'd had at the beginning, such as *How did things come to this?* and *What is she trying to do?* ended up being thrown into his mind's trash bin.

I mean, even I don't know why Itsuwa is so into this! I can't explain what I don't understand! W-well, right now, all I need to do is say thank you to Itsuwa! Fu-ha-ha!! What a marvelous feat—I escaped Index's pursuit without having to get bitt— Urgh!!

Just as he was basking in the glow of victory, Index, angry anyway, bit the back of his head, and he began rolling around in pain. The act made the gorgeous can of cat food splatter all over the floor, and the cat began lapping it up greedily, as if saying, *What a waste!! I'll just have to eat it! All of it!!*

Itsuwa gave a pained laugh and headed into the kitchen. To her eyes, it looked like a heartwarming scene, but for the victim, it was a scene straight out of hell.

Still, though..., he thought. *This was the Amakusa ability to blend in with their environment and all that stuff.* Kamijou looked over to she who had, one way or another, been accepted at some point.

Spread on the floor facedown like an unnatural death with human bite marks in the back of his head, he began to hear the sounds of boiling from a pot and high-pitched sizzling from a frying pan.

I—I get to see a girl cooking, he thought, almost ready to let a tear trickle from his eye.

"Hm? Touma, why do you look like a lamb who just witnessed a miracle?" asked Index.

Kamijou ignored the sister and took in all the blessed light.

Then he started to feel uncomfortable. He was relaxing and letting Itsuwa do all the work. *Maybe I should clean up the room or something*, he thought. Rather seriously, in fact.

Meanwhile, Index, who had vented most of her stress with her Kamijou head bite, started floating toward the kitchen as though drawn by the scent of cooking.

"What?" said Itsuwa. "No, don't eat that fish cake!!"

"Talk all you want—my mouth is past the point of no return!"

Seeing Index, having immediately given in to her own hunger, starting to get in the way, Touma Kamijou rose abruptly. After a fearsome dash, he wrapped his hands around Index's waist and quickly tugged her out of the kitchen space. Then, using the momentum from his lead-up, he hurled her onto the bed with a cry in a strange pro-wrestling throwing technique.

"Don't ruin a man's dreeeeeeeeeeeeeams!!"

"*Mgyuh?!* T-Touma, what was that for?!" she shouted, eyes spinning. The cat kept his distance as though annoyed, but Kamijou wasn't about to give her a real response. Silently, he grabbed Index's head and spun it to face the kitchen. "Look at that, Index!! That is what a freeloader *should* look like!!"

"Ow, ow, ow! Why are you so worked up today, Touma?!"

"Now that I think about it, why are you the 'do nothing but eat, sleep, and watch TV' type anyway?! You'll be working from now on. Go get a sponge and the cleaning spray and clean the bathroom!!"

"Aww, but the Magical Powered Kanamin Integral reruns are about to start!"

"I don't care—just do some work around here already!!"

As Index did nothing but act baffled, Kamijou threw her into the bathroom. Looking at an upstanding citizen like Itsuwa just cleansed your soul. Compared to when others were nearby, like that flame-throwing, cigarette-stinking sorcerer priest or that multi-spy who went "nya, nya" every day of the year, Index seemed relatively "normal." But when he really thought about it, "girl with common sense" was a title he only felt right giving to someone like Itsuwa.

Anyway, I should be an upstanding citizen myself and clean up the room, he thought…But he didn't feel like it was a fair trade, since Itsuwa was making him dinner and he'd messed up the room on his own. *Still better than doing nothing*, he figured—a slapped-together pet theory in the end—before bundling up the open magazines littered about the floor.

And then it happened.

"What…What on earth is that fundamentally Japanese smell?!"

As soon as he heard a girl's sudden cry, there came a *krrrsh-krrrsh* from the veranda that sounded like plastic being destroyed. Kamijou turned, startled, and Itsuwa stopped cooking in surprise; they both saw Maika Tsuchimikado there in her maid clothes.

She must have torn right through the board separating the verandas for each room, which were kindly not supposed to be broken unless there was a fire or other emergency, and invaded.

"You'll pay for that!!" cried Kamijou bitterly. "I was finally feeling clean, like an upstanding citizen, and now another freak shows up!!"

Maika ignored him and sniffed around, getting closer and closer to the kitchen, her normally impassive face seeming extremely focused.

"I smell it, I can smell it! …That miso soup…You're using dried scallops ground to a powder as the secret ingredient, aren't you…?"

"H-how did you know?! Not even my mother ever figured that out!!"

Itsuwa, the chef, was shocked she'd been labeled a gourmet.

Mothers really are the root of all cooking! thought Kamijou, a little sentimental at the hidden domestic word. Meanwhile, Itsuwa, who had just served a small amount of miso soup onto a small plate to test how it tasted, thought for a moment, then, with slow motions, handed the small plate to the girl in maid clothes.

Completely silent, Maika received it with formal gestures like a tea ceremony, bringing it to her lips and pausing for a moment—then *gwaaah!!* Her eyes popped open.

"Th-this woman…She's good…"

"Wh-what?"

"*Gwooorraaaahhhhh*!!" she roared, her tone of voice doing a one-eighty. "This...This cannot stand!!" She went back to the veranda with alacrity and returned to the next room over.

From their open window came the conversation of siblings.

"Wh-what?! Why are you taking away today's white stew, nya?! Wait, what about my dinner?!"

"Quiet, outsider!! Now that I've seen something like *that*, there's no way something like *this* could stand up to it! J-just you wait! Soon, you'll have a taste of *true* miso soup!!"

"What?! I was perfectly fine with that stew just now!!" moaned the blond-haired, sunglasses-wearing agent.

Itsuwa's shoulders perked up ominously. "U-um, have I heard that voice before? In Avignon...? More importantly, what on earth happened to that girl?"

I don't really know, but you probably struck some strange chord to make that maid candidate view you as a rival, thought Kamijou, about to say it before deciding not to. Itsuwa was a decent person. She didn't seem used to weirdos doing odd things around her.

For Kamijou's part, he could only think one thing.

He prayed that she, if nobody else, would remain untainted by these oddballs.

7

For a while, he questioned the relationship between Index and Itsuwa, but once Index ate Itsuwa's cooking, she seemed to completely soften up toward her. Right now, she was idling about the floor, troubling Itsuwa by wanting an eighth helping. The cat, for his part, was having his own fun chewing on a rolled-up hand towel Itsuwa brought.

Kamijou sighed. *Well, at least it didn't turn into major trouble.* If he'd known it was this easy to get Index in a better mood, maybe he'd have to start keeping a constant stock of fish sausages to throw her when she was angry...*Though, no*, he thought, correcting himself; she was sure to bite him as soon as she realized he was hiding treats from her. Nothing ever went that smoothly.

In any case, with dinner done, there was nothing more to do. He didn't have any homework today, and he was never the type to study on his own, so the only things left were to take a bath and go to sleep.

But that was where the problem happened.

"How the heck did you manage to break the bathtub with a sponge and spray cleaner, Index?!"

"B-but I just did what you said! I scrubbed it!!"

As Kamijou and Index's shouting echoed through the night streets, Itsuwa smiled painfully. The three of them had gone out for a simple reason. The bathtub in Kamijou's room (actually, the water heater) was busted and unusable, so they'd ended up walking over to a nearby public bath.

"By the way, I would be willing to bet that you, in fact, did *not* scrub it like poor Kamijou said! And why did I smell plastic melting from the faucet? Because you poured undiluted cleaning detergent all over it! How do you like that detective work?!"

"What? I thought you were supposed to put the detergent on to make it clean."

"Woo-hah! There it is—that wondrous natural confusion of yours!! And thanks to you, the inside of the water heater got burned and almost set the dorm on fire!!"

"Ah...ah-ha-ha. W-well, it's a nice change of pace to use an outside bath once in a while, isn't it?" interrupted Itsuwa with a godlike support play.

Kamijou and Index quieted down. People generally stopped being able to raise hell with someone meekly worrying about them.

Itsuwa flipped through a small notebook. "Academy City has a surprising number of public baths. It has the traditional indoor variety, natural hot springs, and even spa resorts...Oh, why not go here? It's apparently attached to an amusement facility."

"...Wait, Itsuwa, how do you have such detailed information about Academy City?" Even Kamijou, a local, didn't know there were natural hot springs here. And she wasn't holding a guidebook distributed by a city publisher—it was an old notepad, written in so much that it was almost falling apart.

"(...Um, well, getting an understanding of the local geography is crucial when guarding a target...,)" Itsuwa whispered in a barely audible voice. "(And since Acqua is on the magic side, I thought the 'lines' running through the city would help predict how he moves.)"

...It was all well and good that she was passionate about her work, but Kamijou was a little worried. Anti-Skill wouldn't attack before Acqua, in order to follow the rules that upheld secrecy, right? "So where are these leisure baths anyway?"

"Um, it looks like School District 22. This is District 7, so that means it's the next district over."

"School District 22...The underground city?" Despite its status as smallest of all the districts in surface area at about two square kilometers, the super-futuristic spot stood out even in Academy City—which was already sci-fi to begin with—for its development having gone hundreds of meters belowground.

"Hmm," he muttered. "The last train's already gone, though."

Itsuwa continued flipping through her rusty notebook. "It's not very far away. We'll get there soon if we borrow a rental motorcycle with a sidecar. Thankfully, it looks like there's a shop for that nearby, too."

"Wait, you can ride motorcycles, Itsuwa?"

"Well yes, kind of. I can drive cars, motorcycles, small boats...I can't fly an airplane, but I could manage a helicopter..."

She spoke as though she was ashamed. Did it bother her that she couldn't fly an airplane?

"Japan's transit system is highly developed," she continued, "so I don't need it here that much, but...Depending on the job, there could be long stretches of desert or plains nearby."

She wasn't especially bragging or anything. She was squeaking like a fly, as though she'd been scolded for something. Anyway, that would mean she didn't have a Japanese driver's license, but an international one. From Kamijou's point of view, just riding a unicycle was out of this world, so he already had respect for her.

I'm learning a lot of surprising things about Itsuwa the normal girl today, he thought, a little impressed, as they decided to walk into a branch of a motorcycle rental place near the dorms. With all the students in Academy City, there was more demand for them than rental cars, so there were more of these kinds of shops.

Kamijou had a staring contest with the price tag on the motorcycle and eventually gave a frightful face, like he'd been hit by lightning. "I…I see. You're not a student from District 7, so you don't get the local discount!!"

"Um, well, that's fine. I have plenty of funds," said Itsuwa.

But he had the accounting skills of a housewife, and he knew one basic rule: get everything for as cheaply as possible. In the end, they rented a medium-sized bike on a late-night special, mainly for people who missed the last train and couldn't get home. They paid extra to have the sidecar attached.

Itsuwa was the one driving, and Kamijou sat perched behind her. Index was in the sidecar.

"Touma," said Index, "I'm sensing something from how we set this up."

"N-no, you're not. You see, ladies first, a-and the sidecar is the comfiest seat here, so poor old Kamijou had no choice but to give it up," he stated in a suspicious-sounding monotone—the best he could manage, after his heart started pounding as soon as he'd put his arms around Itsuwa.

As Itsuwa tried to be too helpful and push the helmet down over the nun's habit, she suddenly realized something. "Oh. Was it all right to leave your cat at the dorm?"

"We can't exactly bring animals into public baths," said Kamijou. "Our cat is the type to just laze around all the time, so I think he'll be fine."

Incidentally, the calico was currently in front of a super-high-class scratching post Itsuwa had brought with her, trembling and wondering, *C-cypress?! It smells really good for some reason—she's not going to get mad at me if I use my claws on it, right?!* But nobody noticed that.

In any case, once Index mastered the proper way to wear the helmet, Itsuwa started up the motorcycle's engine.

"Oh, wow!" she said. "Academy City sure is empty at night. The steering and the sound of the engine feel good, and the road conditions are clean. I might accidentally start speeding...Maybe we should have bitten the bullet and gone for one of the city's famous superconductive linear cycles. I think I heard that it uses magnetic force to repel the wheels from the housing, thus moving the donut-shaped wheels using electricity or something."

"Well, I don't know much about bikes, but compared to the technology outside...And I'd like to request that you drive safely—*Itsuwa, you idiot! Stop! You're going way too fast!!*"

Kamijou reactively tightened his grip around Itsuwa's stomach, but he wasn't thinking well enough to realize she was happy for the reaction and speeding up because of it.

His dorm was on the edge of District 7. District 22 was adjacent to it and close enough to get to on foot. Itsuwa had brought a motorcycle simply out of consideration that they'd feel cold after the bath and want to get back home quickly.

When they left District 7 and entered District 22, Index's eyes went wide in the sidecar. "Wow, wow! Touma, there's a jungle gym! A humongous jungle gym!!"

District 22's aboveground portion was very different from the other school districts. There were no normal houses and buildings here—it was just lines and lines of wind turbines. And they weren't the electric pole replacements like they were in normal districts, but actual rows and columns of pillars like the cube of a steel building's frame; the propellers stacked upward as well, reaching about thirty stories high. It looked exactly as Index said—like a giant jungle gym.

As they headed for the gate to the underground city, Itsuwa, hands on the handlebars, said, "Since District 22 is all underground, it can't rely on wind power or solar power like the other districts can. Plus, it apparently uses so much electricity that they had to build generators on every little bit of the district to provide enough."

The strangely erudite Itsuwa guided the motorcycle through the squarish gate leading underground.

Beneath the surface, District 22 was a giant standing cylinder, two kilometers in diameter. The road crawled around the outside of the cylinder, spiraling downward as it went. If you put it together with the opposite lane going upward, it would look like the spinning pole in front of barber shops.

The tunnel, illuminated with orange lights, seemed to gently curve around forever. The decorative lighting here was different from normal. Index waved her hands in the air in delight.

Kamijou breathed in the air, tinged with the smell of exhaust. "Underground cities don't go too well with Japan, huh?" he said. "I'd be super-scared of earthquakes and stuff. No matter how strong you make the walls, if the entire fault in the ground moves, it'll all get torn apart, right?"

"They do make a point of claiming their earthquake provisions are perfect, though," mused Itsuwa. "Oh, yes—I believe they say that this spiraling road we're on acts like a giant spring, and when an earthquake happens, it softens the impact."

"...That is a completely groundless rumor. Wait, why do you know about urban legends? They wouldn't even be on the blueprints."

Itsuwa passed this off with an awkward laugh, then said, "By the way, what stratum are these leisure baths on?"

"Um, I believe the third."

"Touma, what's a stratum?" asked Index. "Does it have to do with rocks?"

"No, not that kind of stratum," he said. "They're like floors. District 22 is divided into ten underground strata. And we're apparently going to the third one from the top."

Their conversation went on, and before long, they saw the entrance to Stratum 3, ninety meters belowground. Itsuwa turned on her blinker, decelerated, and turned onto the road leading to it.

Once they went through, the view really opened up. "Wow...!!" Index gaped.

Unlike the orange in the tunnel, this space was a pale blue. It was giant—two meters in diameter, and about twenty meters tall. The ceiling was a giant planetarium screen, giving a real-time display of the starry skies captured on surface cameras. And because the city's illumination was all the same color, it gave the impression to those who entered of bursting straight into the middle of a sea of stars.

Groups of widely spaced buildings towered up as if to break through the planetarium screens, while at the same time functioning as pillars to support this underground city. Of course, the city's roof was a steel frame carriage to distribute the weight, much like a gymnasium's. But apparently, the roof was built so a steel frame was all it needed to support itself. There were several redundant designs in place to support things if it went awry, as well.

Index turned around and around in the sidecar, looking at the scenery. "Are we actually underground? There's a river, too! And a forest!!"

"That forest is apparently an application of hydroponic technologies found inside agricultural buildings," explained Itsuwa. "In addition to purifying the air, it's useful for living as well, for mental health purposes. And the water is ostensibly an important power source in this underground city. It falls to each of the strata in turn, all the while producing water power for them." For some reason, Itsuwa seemed like a tour bus guide to Academy City today.

Index tilted her head. "Itsuwa, why does it need so much electricity?"

"Hmm. The biggest reason is probably the pumps. They have to be able to get oxygen from the surface and then pump the carbon dioxide back out. And they have to purge rainwater and domestic wastewater, so large pumps are indispensable. Forty percent of District 22's electricity consumption supposedly goes into operating the pumps, and it's one of the obstacles to using a place like this for practical purposes."

Most of Academy City's generators relied on wind power, so they could generate however much they wanted without there being much need for worry regarding fuel expenses and environmental destruction. But it didn't work like that in other countries and regions. With environmental issues a much-discussed topic and the price of petroleum increasing by the day, constructing an underground city while having to rely on fossil fuels was realistically too difficult a proposition. Of course, one of the reasons was that unlike Academy City, with its clear city limits, bigger nations with a lot more arable land didn't need to build a city underground.

Well, getting your research to show results and actually bringing it into the market are different issues, after all, thought Kamijou.

Their sidecar-attached motorcycle raced through the man-made ocean of stars. Kamijou, riding in the backseat, pointed to the decorative illumination on a building in the distance they could now see. "Hm? Hey, Itsuwa, are those the leisure baths you were talking about?"

"Oh, I think you're right."

"Isn't that a pretty popular place, though?"

"Well, yes. Apparently, it's third in the city's bath rankings."

...Is that kind of info really going to help guard me from Acqua?

Kamijou had his doubts, but Itsuwa didn't. "What about it?" she asked.

"Nothing...Was just thinking that it's a popular place, so I might run into someone I know."

8

Mikoto Misaka stopped and glanced up at the giant, towering building.

The words PEACEFUL SPRINGS SPA RESORT sat emblazoned on its entrance. The structure stretched all the way from District 22's ground to its ceiling. Broadly speaking, big baths filled the place. There was an extensive lineup of varieties, including several with various medicinal properties, or electric ones, or ones utilizing ultrasonic waves. Nonetheless, it had space left over, which was crammed full of shopping malls, arcades, bowling alleys, and the like.

It wasn't a traditional bathhouse as much as a leisure facility with baths in it. It was designed for a target audience of boys and girls in their teens, too, which made sense because of Academy City's student population.

Thanks to its status as a mainly amusement-based facility, it included VIP baths as well, but Mikoto was after something else.

"...The post-bath Croaker cell phone strap..."

It was a limited-time character item you could get by having ten points on a stamp card. If not for the strap, there wouldn't have been a reason to break her dorm's curfew, sneak out, and shake off her roommate Kuroko Shirai's pursuit.

I mean, bringing her would have been fine, but...Whenever we're at a bath or something, she always pesters me like a coiling snake... Imagining it for a moment gave her a chill down her spine. She shook her head to dispel the unwanted imagery and stormed the bath building. A large hall awaited her on the other side of the entrance, but it had nothing like a reception desk. It was set up so that you paid at the bath entries on each floor.

She slipped by a group flapping fans for cooling off and a group of kids bored of the water and running to the arcade, then headed for the elevator.

"All right," she said, looking at the map on the wall. "Where should I get my stamp today...?"

She'd already been in the ultrasonic wave bath, and electromasters like her couldn't use the electric ones. By process of elimination, she was left with only the ones with heightened basic medicinal properties. It sounded ominous when put like that, but they were simply baths adjusted to have the same effects as outdoor hot springs, analyzed scientifically.

"They should just come out and say they use bath additives...," she muttered bluntly, taking the elevator up. Once there, she paid the fee at the bath's entrance, borrowed a towel, went into the changing room, and quickly undressed. After wrapping herself in the lightly colored towel, she closed her locker and was all ready to head in.

...Unfortunately, this towel is pretty small. A little conscious of her

thighs poking out the edge of the bath towel, Mikoto opened the door to the large bath.

She couldn't feel the building's unique height whatsoever here. There were no windows. It wasn't a scenic place in the mountains—they were in the middle of the city. Putting windows in the women's bath so they could see the scenery would have been suicidal—though of course, this was District 22, so even if it had windows, all anyone inside would see was the regular underground view.

The interior was similar to a typical public bath with separate communal shower and tub areas, but here, the bathing area was split into three sections, each at a different temperature. No paintings of Mount Fuji covered the walls—instead, one wall was taken up by a huge monitor that used colorized magnetic particles. The revolutionary screen's selling point was that you didn't need to use light to display color; you could directly alter the particles for that. Unfortunately, it was absurdly expensive, and normal people had no problems with the screens they'd always used. Tragically, only a few artists and movie theaters had bought any of them.

The monitor appeared to double as a touch screen, and a few younger girls were playing with it. "It's true! I really saw a white angel." "There's no such thing!" "I'm telling the truth. It beat the evil!" they said, putting their hands all over it, drawing pictures. Another woman who looked like she'd come back from the office was watching a nighttime drama on a small window isolated from the rest of the screen.

Mikoto sat down in a corner of the room where the shower faucets were and gently grabbed one of the sensor-equipped heads. After a few seconds, a small monitor at the base of the faucet displayed "38°." The sensor measured her body temperature from her palm, and then—in addition to actually cleaning her—adjusted the water to its most effective temperature for her.

You know, I could have just gone into the tub for a few seconds and left, if all I wanted was a stamp. No, that wouldn't have felt right... Maybe I should have brought Kuroko, dangerous though it might be, and gotten twice the stamps—wait, no, no...?!

As she thought about nothing, she gave herself a light wash with some body soap, then used the hot water to rinse the bubbles off.

But I still only have half the stamps I need. That post-bath Croaker strap is a long way away...

Mikoto didn't actually like baths that hot, so she chose the one section of tub out of the three that was intended for little kids and walked that way.

And then she stopped.

In front of her...

...was a silver-haired, green-eyed sister she knew, soaking in the tub.

"Wh-what?! What the heck are you doing here?!" Mikoto exclaimed.

Index, in the muddy white bathwater, put her pointer finger to her mouth. "...You have to be quiet in the bath!"

She was right, after all, so Mikoto closed her mouth and dejectedly put her foot in.

And then Index piped up again. "...You can't bring the towel into the water!"

Mikoto found herself yielding, a little depressed, to the foreigner lecturing her on Japan's public bath rules. She took off the lightly colored towel and went into the water up to her shoulders, then noticed a unique, unfamiliar girl right next to Index with epicanthic folds in her eyes.

Actually, she wasn't unfamiliar. "Wait, you're the woman that idiot had his face on after that weird soccer ball incident!!"

The sudden cry made the plain girl sputter and her face turn red. She waved her hands around, saying, "N-no, I—I, no, well, I—I!!" trying to make some kind of excuse and failing. Meanwhile, the foreign nun was opening her mouth just a little, her teeth glinting from within.

But Mikoto wasn't listening to the plain-looking girl's words. She glanced at her chest, now less guarded because of her flailing, making an educated guess based on what little she could see from the whitened bath water.

*Bigger than I thought...*She tsked, realizing she'd have to accept her loss honestly. The girl was hidden in the colored water now, but the moment she left the tub it would doubtlessly drive the dagger of despair into Mikoto.

As she watched the plain girl babble on incoherently, probably trying to defend herself, she had a sudden thought.

Did these two know about that idiot's "circumstances"?

His circumstances.

His memory loss.

Mikoto had learned of it very recently. She didn't know anything about it, like how long it had been going on or how it had happened. Based solely on the fragmentary clues she'd gotten, though, it seemed like that idiot wanted to keep the fact to himself...but that was all she could surmise.

Do they...well...Could they know about his amnesia?

She watched them casually, searching for any signs of it, but she wasn't a psychometer; she couldn't read other people's thoughts that easily.

Still soaking in the tub, she thought further. *Wait, this is all that idiot's problem. I don't have a thing to do with it. There's no reason for me to solve anything...and I know that, but ugh, why do I have to worry this much over that idiot in the first place—it's a huge pain, and I can't blub blub blub blub blub blub blub...*

"Wh-what?! Short Hair, you're sinking in the tub!"

"She's gotten dizzy!! We have to help her—quick!!"

"?"

Kamijou, who had gotten out of the bath before the others, was standing in front of a vending machine trying to decide whether to take the milk coffee or ice cream when he suddenly heard footsteps. He turned around.

He saw a female nurse burst out of a room with FIRST-AID OFFICE written on the door and charge into the women's bath, but of course, he didn't know what was happening inside.

9

With this thing and that, the fun-filled bath time was over. Kamijou exited the leisure bath building and stood around at the entrance. Not to smoke, of course—he wanted to feel the night breeze.

"...But I totally forgot we're underground," he said after a while, noticing the state of perfect windlessness, his shoulders dropping.

Disappointed though he was, he had another thought. Acqua of the Back, one of God's Right Seat, the most secret group in the Roman Orthodox Church, had declared war...It was an emergency—and enough of one that it should have been all he was worried about. But now that it had happened, nothing was really happening.

Was it just a bluff...? No, I think it's a little early to decide that, he thought with a groan as Itsuwa, smelling kind of good after getting out of the bath, approached him.

"You'll get the chills if you stand out here," she said.

"Actually, I was feeling a little dizzy, so this is nice."

"Um, we'll be using the motorcycle to get home, too, so considering all that time, you might really get chilly."

Kamijou immediately deflated at the reserved remark.

Itsuwa giggled at him. "Do you want to go for a walk?"

"You're the one who just said I'd get the chills!!"

"If we're going to anyway, we may as well. And after all, can't you get back in the bath again afterward? Several of the baths here seem like pools that you can play in."

That would be a paradise all its own, thought Kamijou, agreeing with her inwardly. To be frank, being in the men's bath by himself had been lonely.

"Oh, right. What should we do about Index?"

"The last I saw her, she was running around the free sample corner in the 'food space' inside."

If he stopped her and invited her for a walk, she was sure to bite him on the spot. He figured she wouldn't be leaving the free sample corner, so she wouldn't get lost.

...Besides, this seems like a good chance to talk about Acqua, too. Acqua of the Back might come to Academy City—and they'd kept it secret from Index. Kamijou was his lone target this time. He didn't want to say too much to her and drag her into a dangerous spot.

With that, he decided to go for a walk in the nighttime underground city with Itsuwa.

The nightscape was almost entirely blue, looking both like the scales of some strange southern butterfly and like an ocean covered with coral. Perhaps because his body was hot after having just gotten out of the bath, it strangely didn't make him feel cold.

"Hey, Amakusa moved from Japan to England, right?" he asked.

"Well, yes."

"What's it like living in England?"

"Hmm..." Itsuwa thought for just a moment. "We did move to London, but they assigned us to a Japanese city block, so it's not all that different. All three meals are the same as in Japan."

"Wait, really?"

"Hmm..." Itsuwa smiled more ambiguously, pausing for just a second. "Well, Amakusa has always been able to learn about any environment and blend in with it. I think, when we're headed somewhere we've never been, we treat it differently than most people would."

That would mean Itsuwa and the others hadn't dragged their Japanese customs there—maybe they'd chosen to stay in a place it wouldn't be strange for a group of Japanese people to hang around. They probably wouldn't care where they went, really, whether it was Japan or the West or China.

"The English Puritan Church is treating us well, too. Our lives are good in London—in an Amakusa way, of course," she added with a smile.

But it couldn't have been that simple. Kamijou had seen their situation several times now. If a political issue arose while they acted on behalf of the Church, the higher-ups would definitely mobilize only

Amakusa members so they could "cut off the lizard's tail," if the need occurred. Becoming affiliated with a huge organization also meant having odd jobs forced upon you.

But Kamijou swallowed all that and just said, "Oh." Itsuwa had more than a smile on her face, but she nevertheless looked satisfied with her current situation. "By the way, Amakusa blends into cities and stuff, right?"

"Yes. That's what we aim for, at least."

"Does that mean…?" he started to say, looking at her outfit again. She was wearing a pink tank top over a brightly colored, sheeplike sweater. Her dark, slim pants had cuts in them that spiraled around the legs, with clear vinyl holding it together to prevent it from flipping up. "Does everyone in London wear clothes like *that*?"

"Oh, um…I tried to pick an outfit that would let me blend in with Academy City…," she said uneasily. "Do I stand out…?"

Kamijou shook his head.

She seemed relieved. "It's hard to explain this sort of thing verbally, but in London, the standard choice of clothing feels a little more mature."

"Huh, I see. I don't know any brands and stuff other than Academy City's. So I guess if you build a wardrobe with a bunch of clothes from over there, then it generally all looks like this?"

"Um, it's not that, exactly. After all, most people in London don't only wear domestic brands. In fact, there are actually cases where it could turn out terribly if I chose my outfit based on that assumption alone…But beyond that, even when wearing the same outfit, it's possible to give off a completely different impression depending on the gestures you use and how you behave."

Itsuwa was muttering at this point. She dealt with all her fashion choices by instinct, so it was hard for her to explain it logically. It was the same as if you asked someone to tell you how to drive a car—most wouldn't be able to give you an answer aside from "you just drive it."

Whatever the case, Kamijou was sort of interested in what Itsuwa wore in London. What immediately came to mind was one other acquaintance he had in Amakusa besides her—Kaori Kanzaki.

"...But aren't Kanzaki's clothes kind of weird?"

"I...?! Wh—? I, you, weird...?"

"I mean, she's mature and everything, but she seems like she's definitely more on the sexy side than mature."

"What a suddenly dreadful evaluation of our Priestess! It's not for the sex appeal; it's so she can build spells, since the lack of symmetry and balance is effective for what she's using, and it's not like she's doing it to show off her curves or anything...!!"

Itsuwa had snapped out of the charm and was now balling her hands into fists in front of her as she launched into her explanation.

Kamijou flinched a little at the late bloomer. "Th-then what? Are you all just gung-ho about being in London? Like it was the right choice?"

Itsuwa seemed dumbfounded by Kamijou's sudden change in topic. "??? Well, we're happy we could go to where our Priestess is," she said. "Um, we've traveled far away, so it *is* a shame we can't see people in Japan whenever we like..." She walked next to him, looking down a little, muttering the next part to herself. "But lately I've started to think maybe that's okay. Kind of like Orihime and Hikoboshi..."

"? What's wrong, Itsuwa?" asked Kamijou blankly.

"N-nothing!! Nothing's wrong, nothing at all!!" she answered, starting to blush all of a sudden and flap her hands in front of her.

10

The current Amakusa team, centered around Saiji Tatemiya, was a short distance away from Kamijou and Itsuwa. They were spread out in a circle around them, securing the main access routes to the pair while continuously matching their pace. Plus, they were completely blending in with the background, without showing any signs of protecting someone. Had an expert bodyguard seen the situation, they would have marveled. And the Amakusa wouldn't even let themselves be known to experts.

Tatemiya, a central figure to Amakusa, which received its orders from the English Puritan Church, was walking down the street in a group made up of a few youngsters (or pretending to be). They proceeded on a route past several karaoke bars and other indoor leisure facilities, pretending to window shop and discuss which place to visit, all the while following Kamijou and Itsuwa at a constant distance.

"What do you think?" asked Ushibuka from next to him.

"About the Itsuwa-pushes-Index-out-of-the-way-for-a-nighttime-date operation?"

"About Acqua of the Back," he responded shortly.

Tatemiya's expression shifted slightly. He gave a casual look around. "No signs of infiltration yet. That's the report we got from Academy City, too."

"…I still don't trust it."

"When you say you don't trust it, you could mean two different things." Tatemiya smirked. "The first is that you simply can't trust Academy City's security when it comes to sorcery. The second would imply the city leaders are scheming, withholding their intelligence from us. Which is it you can't believe in, Ushibuka?"

"Well…"

"The fact that we have three powers—Academy City, the English Puritan Church, and the Roman Orthodox Church's God's Right Seat—plotting against one another over a single high school kid is already strange."

"The Vicar Pope?"

"Yeah, I get it. The name Touma Kamijou means something for Amakusa, too. He's saved us before, and also fought by our side.

"But," said Tatemiya, interrupting himself, "what is Touma Kamijou to Academy City? What is he to the English Church? What is he to God's Right Seat? …Is he alone valuable enough for giant groups like those to mobilize?"

The few around him in the group fell silent for a moment. They knew the answer, and they thought it then but refrained from saying it aloud.

"…We can postulate a few things," said Saiji Tatemiya eventually.

"But is his 'worth' shared among all three of those organizations, even though they're put together differently and spread out in different ways? That's where the ideas stop. I get the feeling there's still a lot we don't know."

"Vicar Pope..."

"If we really want to guard Touma Kamijou, we might need to look into that as well. We've been on the back foot, reacting to the attacks until now. We should directly hit the attackers at home, whoever they are."

That was where he stopped talking. He'd noticed something was wrong.

People were disappearing. At some point, Tatemiya's group had become the only people walking on this nighttime underground street.

Someone had somehow manipulated the flow of traffic. So precisely that even Amakusa, which specialized in blending into crowds, hadn't noticed.

"..." Tatemiya had no words. He signaled with his fingers, and the youngsters with him reached for their concealed weapons.

As they'd been carefully observing their surroundings, Amakusa had felt something.

A sense of oppression.

It was much like the burst of air that came when a subway car arrived at the platform. Something simply huge had come near, and they were feeling its aftereffects.

Tatemiya turned to look that way.

And there was...

11

In that underground city, covered entirely in blue, Kamijou and Itsuwa walked together. The blue was caused by how this city was designed to be scenic from the planning stages, unlike normal cities. The unified nightscape felt somewhat cramped, but as a whole, it was still beautiful.

Itsuwa, walking next to him, suddenly spoke. "No sign of Acqua."

"...I'm sure Academy City security hasn't stopped him. That would be too convenient."

Their relaxing time made it easy to forget their biggest problem at the present moment was still God's Right Seat.

Academy City's police force, Anti-Skill, was no pushover, but Kamijou had seen numerous sorcerers break into the city in the past. He didn't think leaving this in their hands would eliminate the need for worry. In fact, Acqua had broken into the city once already to retrieve Vento of the Front.

The Amakusa reinforcements were reliable, but even there, the implication was that they could only support him so far as they didn't cause a political issue and get cut away with the rest of the lizard's tail. If the English Church wanted to fight Acqua full force, without worrying about how it looked, they would have used Kanzaki without thinking twice.

With the change in conversation, it felt like the very blueness of the city had changed in nature. Whether by unexpected coincidence or what, the color Acqua used was blue, apparently.

"We should be grateful there hasn't been an attack, but...," said Itsuwa, her voice somewhat unsteady. She probably couldn't decide how to take this.

As they progressed through the streets dyed in blue, Kamijou thought a bit. "They might be secretly preparing somewhere in the city or throwing all sorts of complicated things together. Again."

Still, the two of God's Right Seat he'd already fought—Vento of the Front and Terra of the Left—attacked in polar opposite ways. One invaded Academy City to stomp him out in a fair fight, and the other caused worldwide chaos as a roundabout way to strangle the science side.

He couldn't get a grasp on the whole of God's Right Seat with a sample size of two. In fact, both Vento and Terra had been too irritable to use as a reference now.

"We'll just have to keep an eye out for now...," said Itsuwa, clenching a small fist. "Everyone's doing their best, out of sight, including the vicar pope. Come who may, we'll still do the best we can. If we're just doing the same as we always do, we don't need to be especially conscious about it."

"Same as always, huh...?" said Kamijou, a wry grin forming on his lips. "Still, with this crazy God's Right Seat after us, the bathtub breaking and us coming to a leisure facility seems kind of pathetic..."

"N-no, not at all. I don't think so at all," argued Itsuwa, flapping her hands in front of her. "A strong enemy may be after you, but if you're constantly on your guard, it'll wear you out. It's important to keep yourself in peak condition. That way, you can use everything you have when the time comes. Relaxing is actually very efficient in that way. If you try too hard to live in some special rhythm, things never go well. It would be like releasing a freshwater fish into the ocean."

"Is it?" wondered Kamijou aloud.

Their walking route wasn't set in stone. If they talked about Acqua in front of Index, she'd doubtlessly want to fight him. They'd simply decided to keep this all a secret from her. They'd said what they needed to, and they'd just come up to a river; he idly figured they'd cross the iron bridge and return by a different route.

"By the way, where are the other Amakusa people? Like Tatemiya."

"Well, you see...I think they're keeping watch for us a little farther away, even now." Her tone of voice sounded a little disappointed. "...If we had the Priestess with us, too, we'd have the strength of an army."

"You mean Kanzaki, right? I guess she's pretty great, huh?"

"W-well, yes! The Priestess is one of only twenty saints in the entire world! No matter what the problem is, if the Priestess was here, she'd solve it in one fell swoop!!"

"Huh. I see," said Kamijou super-helpfully. "Well, she did fight that archangel, the one with the "Power of God," so she must be really amazing."

"*Bgwehah?!* Fighting...with an archangel? What is that supposed to mean...?!"

"What?" he wondered. It had happened under special circumstances, during Angel Fall; was that why Itsuwa didn't know about it? They seemed to have heard—from Tsuchimikado, most likely—that he'd barged into the changing room while Kanzaki was in there, but…it seemed Kamijou wasn't quite able to get a good mental image of Angel Fall.

He groaned and scratched his head. "Saints and angels sure are amazing. The world is full of amazing people."

"Th-that's a very sloppy evaluation of them…" Itsuwa looked like she hadn't fully recovered from her shock. "But really, between an angel and a saint, angels are ranked higher."

"Is that right? So even Kanzaki couldn't beat one if she tried really hard?"

"Well, that's a difficult question…In terms of raw strength, an angel is definitely stronger. The capacity a single angel has is far, far greater than any powers given to a saint."

According to Itsuwa, there was a limit to how far humans could control saintly powers, and could even destroy themselves if they pushed it too far beyond that. Even scholars in the magic world could only theorize about why angels could store so much power without going berserk. Nobody knew.

"Damn. Whenever I think about studying, my head starts to hurt. Doesn't matter what it is."

"Your evaluation was sloppy, like I said, but I also think you're correct…" Given her drooped shoulders and sigh, she must have been going through a lot herself.

"Back to the topic," he said. "Why we don't have Kanzaki's help, right? Aren't Kanzaki and Amakusa both part of the English Puritan Church? She'd do it if they asked her, wouldn't she?"

"Well…Hmm. She is there, certainly, but saints are like nuclear weapons. I don't think they can have her act outside of England very easily. And she has a history with Amakusa, so we can't easily ask for her help…It's still a delicate problem and all, so…"

As they spoke, they stepped onto the iron bridge. It was about fifty meters long. Not too big as far as bridges went, but considering the entire river was man-made, it was kind of a moving sight on its own.

Its base color, lit up by lights, was blue, as though it were part of the illumination here.

"(...I know I shouldn't let up my caution, but it's just the two of us, and wow...)," she whispered to herself.

"What's wrong, Itsuwa?"

"N-nothing's wrong!! Nothing at all!! Nothing at all is wrong!" She waved her hand in front of her face back and forth at lightspeed. "U-um, well, I was just thinking there don't seem to be many people around. I didn't mean anything by 'just the two of us,' and it's just that it's very prettily decorated, so it feels like a, um, waste, and..."

Kamijou wondered to himself as they went down the bridge's pedestrian lane. Why had she been talking so fast and giving all those fake smiles this whole time?

"Well," he said, "it all depends on the time of day, right? This is what Academy City is like at night. They make the last trains and buses early on purpose, to make it harder to go out at night. I mean, people who want to will anyway, but still."

Despite what he said, a moment later, he felt something was wrong.

The current time was past ten PM. Indeed, major public transport would have been fast asleep by now. It wasn't unusual for the traffic on the roads to change depending on the time—by itself. Especially since 80 percent of the residents in Academy City were students.

However...

A little past ten meant all the night prowlers would be out and about like normal.

Not...good...?!

The landscape was *unnaturally empty.* Kamijou felt a strange chill come over him and went to call out to Itsuwa about the danger.

But he couldn't. He didn't have the time.

"I gave you a warning."

He heard a voice.

From in front of him. The lights on the bridge, blue, symbolizing a certain man: Beyond their halo, in the darkness, came the rough voice of a man.

"You had several options before you."

He heard footsteps.

But they weren't the steps a normal human would make. With every step he took, a dull *znn* rippled along the bridge. A glimpse of overwhelming power. A countdown to death, now distinct. The strange footfalls closing in on them from the blue darkness presented an unfairness that went far beyond brute force.

Itsuwa, faced with the abnormality, was stunned. Her face should have been tenser, thought Kamijou—before immediately wondering what had happened to their connection with the main Amakusa team. Hadn't they been trailing Itsuwa and him from out of sight?

"If you accepted my warning, ruminated on it, and decided it worth entrusting them with your life, then I will, of course, face you head-on."

He smirked.

"But I'll be honest. Was there no better option than this?"

The darkness wiped away.

The only light sources were the dim lamps on the bridge. They hadn't put in lights strong enough to drive back the night. But the man merely stepped toward them from the dimness. That was all he did—and yet it felt as though the darkness had opened up like a curtain to let the man through, then withdrawn.

Brown hair and features like a stone statue. His clothing closely resembled blue golf wear. He looked physically strong but not in a healthy way. His was the body of a blood-soaked soldier.

"You're..."

Kamijou had seen him before. Once—on September 30, in Academy City—he had met this man. This large man, who had swiped Vento of the Front away after Kamijou had just barely defeated her using his Imagine Breaker.

"Acqua of the Back. I believe I've already introduced myself."

God's Right Seat.

And at the same time, one possessing the qualities of a saint.

"Just like you announced you would..."

"I feel no need for intricate plans," said Acqua simply. "I've only come to eliminate the source of the disturbances throughout the world."

You're one to talk, thought Kamijou. Vento of the Front had disabled Academy City's functions. Terra of the Left had thrown the world into chaos. Whatever reasons they might have had, God's Right Seat had no right to tell *him* he was the origin of any disturbances.

"You're not here for talk. You want to kill me right off the bat, don't you?"

"Hmph. Perhaps I was too impetuous."

Irritated, Acqua cast a glance at Kamijou, looking him up and down. "My desire is to sever the origin of these disturbances."

"What are you even talking about?"

"You will not pretend you don't know."

"If anyone caused this, it was you!! You're not going to tell me you forgot what you did at Avignon!!"

"But even that was originally based on our goal of defeating dangerous elements—you, Touma Kamijou, and Academy City."

They weren't getting anywhere, but Acqua didn't even grow angry. That meant he hadn't been listening to Kamijou to begin with.

"The root of all lies in your idiosyncrasy, starting with a certain part of your body. I don't need to take your life—so hold out your right arm. If I sever that now, I will spare your life, at least."

The offer didn't deserve an answer. Acqua knew Kamijou would refuse it.

"What about the rest of Amakusa...?" said Itsuwa suddenly, finally speaking. It must have been some sort of sign; Itsuwa glanced around.

"Futile," said Acqua, his one word cutting her hopes down.

"What have you done to them?" she asked.

"I haven't killed them," he answered simply. "They're not the ones I need to defeat."

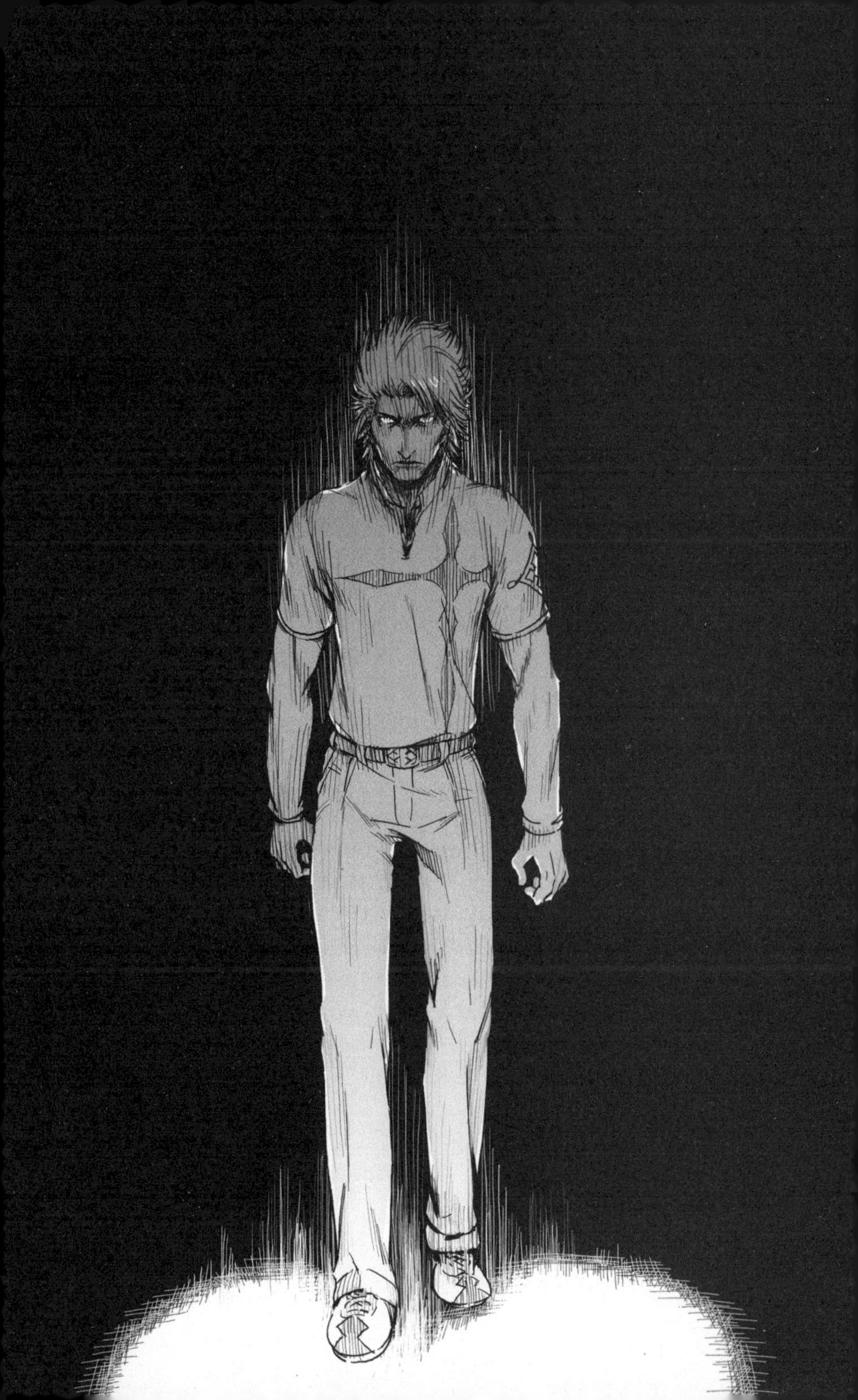

As he spoke, he slowly swayed.

They were ten meters or so apart. As far as Kamijou could tell from watching him, he had nothing like a weapon, and it didn't seem like any were hidden in his clothes. The golf outfit was stretched around his muscles, not giving him any space to stow something inside it.

Nevertheless, Kamijou and Itsuwa focused their minds entirely on him, watching for even the slightest move of a fingertip. Avoiding conflict was an impossibility. Because they were fully aware of that fact, they wouldn't move recklessly and would instead try to gauge the best time to charge in.

However…

From the side.

"?!"

Before Kamijou could even gasp, Acqua had already jumped right next to Itsuwa. He'd disappeared. That was how quickly he'd closed in on her, now deep within striking range. He released an elbow, aiming to deliver a blow to the side of her cheek.

Kamijou didn't hear a noise. But he did just barely make out her body flying over the sidewalk and into the car-less road. He still hadn't taken a breath. Nevertheless, using the air still in his lungs, he reflexively cried out, "Itsuwa?!"

Acqua's voice cut him off. "This isn't the time to worry about others."

Soon, there came a roar.

The source was the shadow extending from Acqua's feet. Like a giant orca leaping from the water's surface, an immense hunk of metal shot out of it. The weapon was over five meters long and resembled the lance a knight would use on horseback.

And yet, it was far different.

The object was put together like a parasol, the framework using iron girders from a building.

It was a metal mace for bludgeoning to death.

"Here I come, my target."

"Urgh!!"

Before Kamijou could prepare himself, Acqua's muscles bulged explosively.

It was no less than a miracle he didn't die. Itsuwa's bag came flying in from out of sight and slammed into him, pushing him in a direction Acqua hadn't predicted.

The five-meter iron ingot, having lost its target, easily tore Itsuwa's airborne bag and stabbed it into the ground like a guillotine.

The bridge was, supposedly, made of asphalt.

But with one heavy *thud*, it rattled. Bolts holding fast to the metal framework began to rupture, making ominous noises. Several of the pale blue lights used for illuminating the bridge went out unnaturally. Kamijou, however, didn't have the time to pay attention to those things. Like a meteorite colliding with the ocean's surface, a barrage of asphalt fragments scattered with Acqua's mace at its center, and some of them had hit Kamijou directly.

"Gaahhhhhhhhh!!"

Just the aftermath made it impossible for him to keep his footing. By the time he felt his feet floating off the ground, he'd already rolled several meters. His back slammed into one of the bridge's support pipes, and only then did he stop.

Clattering.

Fine asphalt shards pouring down like a torrent.

Acqua hefted his mace up to his shoulder—it looked like a bundle of metal beams—and took a step toward Kamijou where he lay.

The dust coiled around Acqua, as though it were his fighting spirit made visible, and blew about.

Then, with only his eyes, he looked to the side.

Itsuwa had staggered to her feet. She had put together her Friulian spear, which could be taken apart to store in a bag—she'd probably taken it out before throwing the tote—and had its cross-shaped tip pointed at Acqua.

But she'd taken considerable damage from the first attack. A trickle of red blood dripped from her lips, and her cheeks had reddened. Her aim wavered more unreliably than a fishing pole in the wind.

Acqua didn't even laugh. He just spoke. "The lot of you together couldn't stand up to me. Did you think just one could challenge me and win?"

"...I...still have my pride."

How much emotion, how much determination must have been behind those few words?

In response, Acqua simply responded, "I see."

That was all.

Shit...!! Kamijou tried to force his pained body to move, to get between Itsuwa and Acqua. But he couldn't move the way he wanted. And in the meantime, Itsuwa and Acqua clashed at short range.

Itsuwa moved quickly—but Acqua had already vanished. The next thing he knew, the side of Acqua's metal pipe mace was buried in Itsuwa's side. Acqua continued turning himself, using centrifugal force to swipe the mace, with Itsuwa on it, in a horizontal arc at Kamijou.

His brain didn't even have time to consider reacting.

The original weight of the heavy metal mace added to an entire person's body weight was more than enough to hold Kamijou down, resting against a metal beam as he was. It forced all the air from his lungs. He tasted metal. For a few seconds, his stricken body left the ground. A moment later, the damage hit him so hard it felt like the earth's gravity had been multiplied, and he crumpled to the ground.

Itsuwa, lying on top of him, didn't move. He couldn't even get the limp girl off him.

As his consciousness hazed, he managed to make out Acqua of the Back as he descended upon them.

He's...too far beyond...

Vento of the Front and Terra of the Left—their movements had at least been visible. He could slip past their attacks and counter, even damaging them in return.

But...what in the world is this guy?

Acqua of the Back.

Was he really a human like Kamijou?

This wasn't a difference between two people. It felt like going up against an MMORPG character over a hundred levels higher than you. It wasn't that he was using some cheat to prevent attacks from working. His abilities were just so much greater that it wasn't even a fight. How was he supposed to beat him?

"Your right arm," said Acqua, slowly lifting his mace overhead. "If you offer it, I will spare your life."

"Screw...you..."

He tried to get up, but he had no energy. More and more, he was realizing his limits, but he didn't give up, still trying to muster every ounce of strength.

But...

"I see," said Acqua. "In that case, I'll give you another taste of reality."

12

Urgh...

Itsuwa had passed out for just a moment.

The first thing she noticed as her consciousness seeped back into her was the stench of metal. Next was the pain. Immediately after sensing the pain in the core of her head, a wave of agony washed over her like a tsunami. Surprisingly, her vision and hearing, normally her most reliable tools, lagged behind the most.

Faintly lit darkness.

Blue despair burying her.

Several nearby metal beams were split apart, the asphalt was shattered, and sand flew about the bridge.

A tragic scene—the nightscape she and Kamijou had just been walking through, now torn asunder.

And the feeling of a spear grip in her hand.

"?!"

Finally remembering what had happened, Itsuwa hastily tried to push herself off the ground.

Then her palm touched something slimy.

It was warm and stunk of iron enough to make her head spin. Most of all, it was colored a deep red. The fluid had a simple identity.

Fresh blood.

But Itsuwa hadn't shed this much. Actually, if she had, she probably wouldn't have been conscious right now. It wasn't ink, or any other liquid, either. It was doubtlessly human blood.

Whose blood was it, then? Her mind immediately tried to reject it.

She barely needed to think.

It was Touma Kamijou.

"Awake, are you?"

Thinking calmly, Itsuwa determined Acqua of the Back, weapon in hand, should have still been standing right in front of them.

"If you are, then move. My attack will deliver far too much force. If I'm not careful about unleashing my full strength, it will cause collateral damage."

But Itsuwa wasn't thinking about him. Her shoulders trembled madly as she slowly, slowly turned around to look behind her.

To see what she'd been leaning against the entire time she was out.

Kamijou's arms and legs, limp, without energy. His face was splattered with red. His eyes, neither fully open nor fully closed, were half-open, like a broken autofocus. The pain searing through him would have felt like he was being ripped apart. Despite that, he didn't move a muscle.

Was he alive? Was he dead?

She didn't even know that.

She was so close to him, but merely knowing whether he was alive or dead was out of her reach.

"Ah…ah…"

Her ability to make decisions shattered.

She'd forgotten entirely about Acqua of the Back, the immediate threat. Despite being in front of her enemy, she moved her hand soaked in the blood of another, clawed up the nearby scattered asphalt fragments, took out a hand towel, and removed the wallet from Kamijou's blood-soaked pants pocket.

The Amakusa-Style Crossist Church didn't use odd incantations or Soul Arms in their sorcery.

All they needed were common, ubiquitous life necessities.

Itsuwa rebuilt the occult vestiges hidden inside such items to try to cast healing magic that would stop the blood flowing out, close his wounds, and replenish his vitality. For the girl, the "problem" and the "battle" had focused to a single point: whether this boy lived or died.

In actuality, in spite of the chaos roiling within, her actions were surprisingly precise and swift.

She cast the healing spell in the blink of an eye.

Faint, dim orbs of light floated up from Kamijou's limp, unmoving body. The green glow was reminiscent of fireflies. The lights squeezed into the gaps in his skin, burying themselves in the tears.

But…

Then she heard a *bam!!*

The healing magic she'd just built vanished without a trace, blown to smithereens.

The cause was clear.

"…Ah…"

With unsteady movements, she looked away from his face to the right hand hanging at his side.

His right hand.

The Imagine Breaker.

The unique power that nullified all unnatural phenomena, whether good or evil.

"*Uwaaaaaaaaaaaaaahhhhhhhhhhhhhhhhhhhhhh!!*"

Itsuwa screamed and rebuilt the once-destroyed healing spell. But it was futile. As soon as she cast it, the sorcery was broken—and again she built it, and again it was destroyed. Though she was using necessities you could find anywhere, if she kept wasting them like this, it wouldn't be long before she ran out. The next thing she knew, there was nothing left to use for the spell.

"Finished?" called Acqua as Itsuwa continued her struggles.

But Itsuwa wasn't able to give a real answer.

All she could do was keep screaming. Acqua didn't say any more to her.

Wordlessly, he swung up his big leg, then buried it into Itsuwa's curled back.

Crack!! came a roaring noise, and her screams stopped.

With the violent sound, the energy left her limbs. She'd been knocked out.

"Hmph."

Without a glance for the crumpled Itsuwa, Acqua lifted his giant mace again.

His original job.

His target—the unconscious Kamijou's right shoulder.

But he didn't bring the mace down.

No, he hadn't felt mercy.

No, it was Itsuwa—wounded all over, damage having accumulated to her very core, who should have been out cold—who slowly, unsteadily worked her hands, grabbed her spear, and shot up to her feet.

As though standing as a wall between him and Kamijou, curiously enough.

"Guh, ngah, *oooooooooooooooohhhhhhhhhhhhhhhhhhhhhhh!!*"

Her roar, which rattled his organs, was genuine mortal desperation. She didn't care about her chances of victory anymore. One look at her bloodshot eyes, and he could easily guess she no longer had that luxury.

She couldn't let him die.

She couldn't let him be taken from her.

She needed to stand up.

But that was all—she simply moved.

As she coughed up a clump of blood, a tenacious light came to her eyes that hadn't been there before.

Acqua sighed tediously.

At the same time, the arm gripping his mace slowly expanded. His hand grasped its handle with terrible force of muscle, so tightly that even though it was made of steel, he might break it.

Acqua hadn't acknowledged Itsuwa as an enemy.

He was simply about to crush both his obstacle and Kamijou to pieces in a single strike.

Itsuwa bit her lip.

She knew how carelessly he was treating her.

And she knew the difference in their strength was enough to call for such treatment.

"..."

Itsuwa stayed silent for a moment.

Not only did her mouth remain still—her mind was quiet. A curious blank in her heart, with nothing in it. Was it a sort of determination, or was it resignation? A moment later, when she regained all her thoughts, she turned her wobbling spear, pointing it clearly at Acqua.

It was nothing less than a declaration of war made by one about to meet her maker.

What little strength remained within her focused to a single point.

Suddenly, the silence broke, and the end came.

"Thank you, Itsuwa."

However, Acqua's strike was not what had shattered her will.

It was the weak hand of a certain boy laid upon her shoulder from behind.

Her slight body shivered at his few words.

She couldn't turn around.

The hand on her shoulder had to be ripped up.

But the only thing Itsuwa saw in her mind was a gentle face.

"I feel a little better thanks to your healing spell."

That was impossible. His Imagine Breaker destroyed all magic. Itsuwa's healing spell couldn't have had any effect.

The boy's voice, too, was faint, as though wrung from his throat. His voice wavered unreliably, sounding like it could vanish at any moment.

Despite all that, those few words had a warmth to them.

She almost let herself collapse, but then she realized what the boy was thinking, and a chill ran down her spine.

Why had he stood up now?

Why did he force himself to stand up when even moving a finger was too hard?

And what did he have in mind by putting his hand on her shoulder to stop her right before leaping at Acqua of the Back?

“Wa—!!”

She didn’t have time to call out.

The boy put strength into the hand on her shoulder, then pushed her forward as though trading places with her. With her will already broken, her body, held up by mental force alone, fell limp.

“Ooooooooooooohhhhhhhhhhhhhhh!!”

He may have been an amateur when it came to battle, but he at least knew he couldn’t beat Acqua.

That wasn’t his goal.

Acqua of the Back said from the start that his only target was Kamijou. He said he hadn’t killed the main Amakusa team deployed nearby. If the battle reached a conclusion quickly, it would decrease casualties.

For example…

Itsuwa, directly next to him, wouldn’t have to die.

“…!!”

Itsuwa’s face distorted. All she could do was stare at his back. Clear liquid began to fall from her eyes. She shouted something, but Kamijou didn’t turn around. He remained facing forward and jumped straight toward Acqua.

“You have guts,” the man said simply.

And then, before her eyes, he unleashed a tremendous attack. He swung that giant mace, over five meters long and made of steel, horizontally, slamming mercilessly into the boy’s side. A roaring noise pierced her ears, one that you wouldn’t think came from a person. The boy, now caught between the mace and a metal bridge pillar, fell completely limp. He couldn’t even throw his fist, clenched with desperate determination, at Acqua.

He fell, this time perfectly unconscious, his body leaning over the giant mace. He looked like a futon hung out to dry. Acqua smiled.

As if to praise the defeated for his struggle.

"You have one day."

With the unconscious boy still caught on his giant mace, he swung it slowly using one arm.

"To tear him apart now, without anesthesia, would be inhumane. Prepare him an artificial arm—or whatever you like. If he says he will give us that arm, that root cause of the disturbances, in that time, then I will spare his life."

With that, Acqua heaved his mace with reckless ease, swinging it to the side.

A monstrous attack from one who was both God's Right Seat and a saint.

The boy's body, caught on the mace, flew away from the bridge with the speed of a cannonball. He passed over the railings, plunged several hundred meters straight away, collided with the dark, cold water's surface, and then, instead of sinking, bounded back up. The incredible speed caused his body to skip off the surface again, then a third time, until he finally sunk underneath next to a cruiser, sending a bomblike blast of river water everywhere.

Splosh!! came the roaring noise a moment later.

Without checking to see if he was alive, Acqua of the Back turned away from Itsuwa.

And finally, he repeated this:

"You have one day."

INTERLUDE ONE

What, can't get to sleep?

Then let's have a talk, grandpa to grandson. Hm? My stories are long and boring? Well then, they'll put you to sleep, right?

Let's see. Maybe I'll tell you about the Astrologers' Brigade.

Oh, right. Yeah, that's what they used to call us. We still do the same thing, basically. That's right. It's like what you do, helping people any way you can. We're technically a Crossist sorcerer's society. We go out and listen to all kinds of people, then secretly use magic that helps the situation. That's the kind of people we are.

But a long time ago, we had a lot more requests than we do now. I'm not lying! Everyone in the country relied on us. So many people would gather that we couldn't keep them all in one place. Grandpa and the others had to take a nice, slow trip around all of Russia because of that.

Unfortunately...Well, trouble happens wherever you go.

Some troublesome people started watching us.

No, no, no, no. Just to be clear, not all Russian Catholics are bad people. It's just that one idiot decided he'd take possession of an entire branch of the Russian Church. That's how we ended up getting chased around by professional battle groups.

What was the idiot's name?

What did they want to do after they captured your grandpa?

I can't tell a brat like you something like that. Whatever way you slice it, we're still talking about state secrets. It would be easy to say, but they won't go easy on you, even if you're a kid. Anyway, I can't just go spouting it out wherever I want.

In any case, the people the Russian Catholics sent after us were very stubborn. It was a serious group of monsters made to fight things that weren't human, like ghosts and fairies. We were only there as helpers, so we wouldn't be able to fight them in a real battle. They were too much for us.

We decided to flee the country instead. The one fortunate thing was that they were Russian Catholics. That meant if we could get across Russia's borders, we'd manage. Hope sure is an amazing thing. People will work as hard as they need to for a handful of straw.

But it was a terrible wasteland there. Negative fifty degrees. And dozens of kilometers to go to the border. Boy, was it tough! How do I put it—the way it felt was like a world away from pain. All we could feel was our feet growing heavy. We walked a very long time like that. Everyone walked equally—old people like your grandpa and rascals even smaller than you. And you were in your mommy's belly at the time. That is probably why she's strong as a bull.

What's that? Wouldn't the Russian Catholic people after us have had just as hard a time?

No. They were trained to move in eternal tundra like those. They were real professionals. The way they moved around was steady, like machines or puppets. Not only were they first-rate; their equipment was top-of-the-line stuff, too. They used horses made of metal. Eight-legged ones, if I remember. Ah, yes. A kind of Soul Arm—code-named Sleipnir, if I recall.

It was clear as day which of us was faster—us or the Russian Catholics.

We could just barely make out the Russian border through the blizzards. But we knew. We knew the Russian Catholic pursuers would catch us before we got there. Our hope was visible but unreachable. Their shadows were quickly getting closer, but we couldn't do anything about it. Anyone would decide to give up then.

It would have been easier to take a knee than to work hard for nothing, right? But we couldn't do it. Once the border was before our eyes, we couldn't even give up.

Hmm? What happened after that?

Well, we managed to get away, of course. If not, I wouldn't be here, and you wouldn't have been born. What part of it is bothering you?

Oh, I see, I see. You don't know how we shook off the Russian Catholic Church's very finest.

That one's easy.

Someone appeared before us then.

Someone named William Orwell.

CHAPTER 2

Those Who Rise from Defeat

Flere210.

1

Noises bustled through the hospital that night.

This was the emergency care hospital on School District 22's seventh stratum.

The small wheels of a stretcher carrying a patient clicked and clacked. Several emergency rescue workers advanced in a ring around it as the sounds ventured from outside into the building. The rescue workers' hands pushing the stretcher passed it off to doctors and nurses, then the stretcher entered a concentrated care room before finally disappearing through the door of an operating room.

"...We're done, somehow," said a young male doctor some time later, watching the stretcher come out of the operating room and go back into the concentrated care room. "I can't honestly say he's in stable condition, but..."

The hospital hallways were lonely now that visiting hours had ended. However, several figures did populate the dimly lit passage. Many, even. Young and old, male and female, about fifty in all, leaning against walls and sitting on couches as they listened to the doctor's words. The majority of them were adorned with torn clothes and bandages. Quite a few even had a distinct redness seeping through the white cloth.

They called themselves Amakusa, but the young doctor didn't know what organization they were referring to, exactly. If he were to put it bluntly, they were an awfully suspicious bunch, but occasionally you'd get these sorts of throngs of delinquent boys inside if a Skill-Out leader was hospitalized. Given that, the doctor made a point not to ask any more questions.

"Speaking broadly, if he was a normal person, I would tell you he needs absolute quiet to rest. Going into more detail—first, bruises all over and a concussion. Next, dislocation of the right shoulder and left ankle. Finally, pressure on his internal organs..."

"...Meaning you can't make a call, right?" asked a tall man with beetle-like glossy black hair, choosing his words carefully.

The doctor let out a heavy sigh. "There is one piece of good news, I suppose...The scariest thing was the possibility of oxygen deprivation, because he was underwater for such a long time...but it seems the damage was minimal."

The young doctor continued, looking at what seemed to be medical records in digitized form. "Still...Despite several eyewitness accounts, the root cause isn't something I can believe out of the blue. A human body being blown hundreds of meters over a bridge, then skipping off the water like a rock before slamming into it... The situation by itself is unbelievable, but the fact that he staggered to his feet amid the worst of a disaster like that is strange, to say the least."

"He was going easy...," muttered someone from the dark hallway.

The doctor turned that way, but he couldn't tell who'd said it. They were an odd group. So many of them all together in the hospital stood out magnificently, but nobody was individually conspicuous. It looked like a scene of a random crowd of people. And that was despite close to fifty of them being bandaged up.

"Anyway," started the beetle man—the only conspicuous one of their number—asking the doctor, "this doesn't mean it's all over, yeah?" just to make sure. "If he can talk, I'd like to give him a quick apology, if I could."

"Wh-what are you saying?! He needs complete bed rest! A-and I don't know what you want to apologize for, but that's not a good idea right now. He's asleep from the anesthesia. And even without its effects, he probably wouldn't have the stamina to wake up. We need to let him rest for the moment." The doctor indicated the concentrated care room with his jaw. "And besides..."

In order to make it easy to see changes in patients at a glance, even from outside, the intensive care room had glass panes for walls, and they could see several patients asleep from the hallway. On one of the beds, ringed with a cluster of machines, lay a spiky-haired boy.

The beetle man glanced that way at the doctor's suggestion. His face clouded slightly.

As though nestling against the bed, or as though kneeling on the floor, was a girl. A girl in a white habit, gripping the patient's palm, enfolding it with both hands.

Index.

"...My experience as a doctor tells me to let them be," cautioned the young doctor, having eliminated the emotion from his face.

The beetle man didn't seem to have the guts to go inside and interrupt, either. After he nodded quietly, the doctor walked away down the hallway.

The beetle man—Saiji Tatemiya—took just one step away from the glass wall of the patient's new room.

It frustrated him to no end, but there was nothing he could do for the boy. None of the healing or recovery magic handed down in Amakusa would work. All he could do was pray for his safety—and he didn't know if he even had the right to do that.

They'd told him they'd protect him from Acqua of the Back, but they'd been literally kicked to pieces. Routed. Tatemiya and the others were in shambles after the man's attack, which felt almost like a quick side job. They each fell to the ground as Acqua moved toward his target, and they could do nothing but watch him go.

On top of that, at the end, the person they were guarding fought to defend his Amakusa "friends"...and this is how he ended up. Bandages wrapped around his whole body, gauze plastered to his skin. A civilian wouldn't have been able to tell, but it was plain to see from a sorcerer's point of view. Even their blending in to the environment, like in peacetime, had thinned.

Amakusa had lost—to everything.

They'd lost to Acqua of the Back, and more importantly, they'd lost to Touma Kamijou.

"...Damn it."

Tatemiya gritted his teeth. Battered though they were, the enemy wouldn't wait. According to Itsuwa, Acqua of the Back said if they didn't let him sever Touma Kamijou's right arm and take it before a day was up, Acqua would attack Kamijou again. Obviously, they couldn't let either of those happen—his right arm being taken or him being attacked.

They knew what they had to do.

They had to stand up and face anything in order to protect Kamijou.

"And why are you curled up like that?" asked Tatemiya.

In a corner, which had even less light than the dimly lit hallway, making it practically a lump of blackness, he sensed something like a small animal giving a start.

It was difficult to tell without looking closely.

But it was Itsuwa there, without a doubt, making herself small on the couch.

Bandages on her limbs, a square piece of gauze covering her right cheek. It looked incredibly painful, but it was her mind that had been shattered, broken so badly her physical wounds couldn't compare.

"...I...I..."

Her voice was shaky and punctuated by a hiccup. A sob. She'd already shed so many tears that she couldn't control her diaphragm.

"...I said...I said I'd protect him. My spear, my magic...None of it helped...But he said...he said thank you...I couldn't protect him at all. I couldn't even get a single hit in as Acqua walked away...But he thanked me..."

He could hear the sound of falling drops. It may have been tears, or it may have been blood from her palm, from her clenched fist.

"When...When I heard about him, I thought, *What amazing power he must have.* But I was wrong. He can't rely on any defensive spells. No matter how much healing magic I use, I can't even fix a glancing wound. He truly was fighting unarmed, and yet I..."

"Itsuwa..."

"I left him to suffer and did nothing."

At that point, Itsuwa might have been smiling. As she sniffled, he could see a twist in her face that looked like one.

"Why is someone like that living such a carefree life by herself? There's one odd person among the victims, so why isn't she stricken by divine judgment?! This doesn't make any sense. I should have been the one sleeping in that bed!! That would have solved everything!!"

Her sentences wavered between strength and weakness. She was confiding in them, talking to herself, repenting, venting, complaining, and howling like a beast—all at the same time.

She didn't have a full grasp of her own emotions.

She was so cornered that she couldn't give them any thought.

Tatemiya narrowed his eyes slightly when he realized that, then stepped toward Itsuwa, splitting the dark shroud.

"You gonna stand up?"

"..."

"What the heck are you doing anyway?" he asked lightly, but then he grabbed Itsuwa's collar with a hand. Before anyone could say anything, he lifted her with fearsome strength and slammed her against the nearby wall.

A dreadful *thud* echoed through the hallway.

The impact shot through Itsuwa's back, making it hard to breathe. But she didn't put up any sort of resistance. She just gasped for oxygen, glaring back at Tatemiya with tear-soaked eyes.

"...too, you...," she managed to say between breaths. "Tatemiya, you lost, too..."

"..."

She knew how ugly her words were. And that she shouldn't have been venting her anger on Tatemiya. But she still pierced him with what she said—because her mind couldn't endure any more without doing it. This girl, Itsuwa, truly wanted to protect the boy. She earnestly desired to fulfill her promise. And those feelings had been shattered to pieces by overwhelming force. They were precious, something Itsuwa alone needed to understand.

But instead of all that, Tatemiya said, "He risked his life to save someone like this?"

Itsuwa's eyes widened at the remark. She looked like he'd stabbed her with a knife. Her face hadn't betrayed any pain even when he'd slammed her against the wall, but now it was filled with a twisted agony.

"Roughed up in front of your friends, in front of the one who saved your life and got wrecked for it...And you still do nothing. That kid seriously sacrificed himself for the likes of *you*? What a waste of life. It's a dog's death, is what it is. Hah. Pretty simple when it comes down to it, eh? This was just some idiot saving an idiot and doing something idiotic."

Itsuwa's face flushed with heat. Still being held up, she let out an animal-like roar and tried to throw a punch at Tatemiya. Before she could, though, he took her body from the wall it was up against and swung her down to the floor.

There came a rumble so loud it sounded like an earthquake.

He remained towering over Itsuwa, who was now having difficulty breathing again, and looked into her eyes. "Listen up. You don't seem to understand this, so I'll spell it out for you."

His voice was low. Very low.

Fires of anger smoldered in Saiji Tatemiya's tone.

"Acqua of the Back *will* return."

Itsuwa gave a start.

Tatemiya forced her to think about the facts again—he knew them so well it made him want to pretend he didn't.

"While we're here worrying ourselves to death, the time limit keeps ticking down. Our lives already have a low chance of continuing, and with every second we waste, it gets a whole lot lower! Are you going to let that happen? There's still a chance. However small it may be, there's still a chance. And you're going to throw it all away because of your bullshit regrets and guilt?! You're going to give up and let his right arm be cut off before he knows the difference?! If you want to protect his smile, then get up. Don't throw away someone else's life just because it's convenient for you!"

His shouting was practically a roar.

Itsuwa said nothing, so he continued, "If help came whenever we asked, we'd already be doing that. If someone told us our saint—our Priestess—would come, we could leave the rest to her. But that's too good to be true. It's impossible. Listen here—Acqua of the Back is absolutely going to return. Are you willing to make this hospital into a battlefield? All because you wanted to escape reality?!"

"Tate...miya..."

"You can stay quiet all you want, but Acqua won't stop!! Even if we ask for help, the English Church won't change their plans and send some nice little reinforcements!! All that's left is for those who can move to move. We're the only ones here who can fight!! We may be pitiful, but if we don't do something now, who is going to protect that kid?! He's still under the effects of anesthesia!! Don't you get it?!"

The hand gripping Itsuwa's collar cracked. He was holding on to it so strongly, he could have destroyed his own hand. And Itsuwa knew—she wasn't the only one feeling angry, ashamed of herself. All of them had tried to protect Touma Kamijou, all of them had failed, and all of them accepted it.

They would still rise again.

They felt the shame of defeat, but instead of falling to their knees, they would rise.

To protect what was important to them.

Then...

I...I'm...

"You want to apologize to him?" he said, looking into her eyes. "You want to help that kid you're supposed to protect? The one in there, all messed up? You want to get him back out into the sunlight?"

Itsuwa forgot to cough, even, and nodded slightly. She said something, but a sob made it indiscernible.

"...Then fight. Prove to him you're the best woman out there. Let him know it was a good thing he risked his life for you. Apologies or smiles—no one can do either without being alive. Unless you want to repent in front of his grave, all we can do is fight."

Tatemiya took his hand from her collar and slowly rose. He looked around, then asked the others, "Are there any other idiots who think like Itsuwa here?"

His voice carried through the hallway, as if thoroughly demolishing the depressed atmosphere brought on by their regret and powerlessness.

"If there are, then step forward. I'll wake you up."

Nobody answered.

But everyone was prepared.

Their regret and their sense of powerlessness hadn't disappeared—they just had something stronger: the will to fight.

Tatemiya looked among his nearly fifty comrades gathered in the dimly lit hospital hallway and said, "If not, then fine. Now we just have to give this everything we have."

The members of the Amakusa-Style Crossist Church wouldn't turn back.

They left the boy and the sister in the intensive care unit and headed off to battle against a strong enemy again.

"Seriously. Someone right in front of us who can't be saved? I expect everyone to reach out and help."

There was only one thing to do.

Their king was in check, so they needed to turn the tables and protect the boy's life.

2

Acqua of the Back lingered in the night's darkness. He was in a forested park on a street corner some distance away from District 22's third stratum urban district. His reason for being here was simple—he wanted to distance himself as much as he could from the artificial objects of scientific technology flooding the place. Of course, now that he'd realized even these woods were science themselves, an application of hydroponic technology, he was currently in low spirits.

The whole underground must be a space entirely created with machinery.

A starry sky hung above him, but even that was an illusion of planetarium screens. Anyone with a little knowledge of magic would have spotted the difference.

Lighting here was sparse, as if to keep expenses low. One small, square light, however, shone in the darkness: Acqua's cell phone.

He was talking to the Roman Orthodox pope. Their phones, though, weren't powered on. The glow on the tip of the antenna was the glow of magic.

Even with this, we can't be sure nobody is listening in. Amakusa, was it?—those English Puritan vanguards seemed to have been here as well.

Still, it was better than stupidly using a phone inside the grand headquarters of the world's science faction.

"*I have to say,*" said the pope, "*I hadn't thought you'd stop short of killing him and only take his arm. I believe Vento of the Front told me that those in God's Right Seat never changed their philosophies.*"

"That's because Vento has personality issues. In actuality, we must be flexible in each situation, ready to take action as circumstances demand...Of course, in Terra's case, he took it too far."

Acqua had been the one to butcher someone in his group and send his corpse to enemy organizations, but he didn't seem to feel regret or guilt over it.

"The reality is," he continued, "that the boy's uniqueness is focused in his right arm. Stealing that means removing the threat. We don't have the time to be absorbed with a single young man."

"*Personally, I prefer it that way as well,*" said the pope on the other end. Acqua thought he heard him smile. "*I said this to Vento earlier as well, but...Destruction is the only choice for enemies of God who have clearly become such by their own volition—but I hear the boy in question does not yet know God. To be honest, I have qualms about simply killing him. Of course, Vento snorted when I said that.*"

"...I don't know what you expect from me," said Acqua, voice level, "but I'm neither as upright or altruistic as you. If the time comes when I must kill him, I will do so. Now is not that time. If that time does come, I will merely kill him. I'm sure there is a future in which that time doesn't come, should several choices and strokes of luck align. That is all this is about."

He wasn't lying. Only four people were part of the world's highest organization. Terra of the Left, one of those few, had been swiftly murdered—by Acqua of the Back's hand. If the boy was no longer hostile after his right arm was gone, that was fine. If he was, or if he refused to proffer his arm—the rest was simple.

Acqua would erase him.

It was so simple when put into words, and the single strike he needed to send the boy to his grave would be even more curt than his words. Because Acqua had the power. He had the resolve. And even knowing that, his face remained stone cold.

"*Such an odd situation,*" said the Roman pope abruptly. "*God's Right Seat was established as advisors to generations of popes, and now it has trodden into the center of enemy territory while I, the pope, observe from the Vatican.*"

Crossism was a monotheistic religion.

They had but one God, and all miracles were centralized and managed around that one God. He was absolute, so nobody could resist him. Originally, all the world would have been filled with happiness, and no unhappy people would have ever appeared.

However, what was the reality?

A glance through history showed it clearly: The failure of the Crusades, the spread of the Black Death, the expansion of the Ottoman Turks. It was far from people being happy or not—the entirety of the European continent faced several turning points where it could have been annihilated.

It was too much for a single pope. But as the symbol of a religion holding up their God as absolute, the very act of consulting with another would, in a way, be scandalous.

That was why God's Right Seat was created. A special group of consultants riding alongside Crossist society's pyramidal structure, seeking to have such knowledge and power that even a pope could rely on them as needed.

Cardinals, consuls, tacticians—completely different from all these, people who didn't actually exist inside that pyramid, carrying out the role of providing voiceless advice.

It always had four seats. The members of the Right Seat corresponded to the four archangels, who were especially important angels. Their existence had continued by switching out one after another—the "contents" only—in accordance with its need.

Still, perhaps at times, despite the terrible situations, the popes had relied overmuch on their shadow advisors. At some point, the Roman Orthodox Church had fixed itself around God's Right Seat at the center.

Acqua thought about it only for a moment. But he made no mention of it in his words. "The next time I contact you will be after it's finished. Leaving aside whether the target lives or dies—"

Suddenly, a loud noise interrupted him.

It was the air.

Something had blinked, as if blending in with the darkness. It was such a small light that a normal person's sensory organs would not have been able to pick it up. Acqua detected danger there. Leaving the cell phone between his shoulder and ear, he took an easy leap backward.

The air swirled of its own accord, then the space Acqua had just been standing in was gouged out along with the ground, shaved away and vanished.

Acqua furrowed his brow at the odd phenomenon and eventually came up with a guess. *They're spreading some sort of fine particles into the air, ones that dismantle objects.*

If he had been well versed in science, he would have considered Bowing Images, nano-sized reflective alloys. They were ultra-small grains without circuitry or a power source that showed a specific reaction to particular frequencies. It was like using a TV remote control to operate a radio-controlled car—except to tear off singular cells in creatures.

As Acqua was watching for the unseen power, another change occurred, this one in the giant planetarium screen making the artificial night sky. With a shrill *buzz*, a warning message began to transmit in the entire stratum.

"Anoxic warning issued for all of Stratum Three. All citizens must either quickly evacuate to buildings designated as disaster countermeasures or equip household oxygen tanks. We repeat. Anoxic warning issued for all of Stratum Three..."

"I see." Acqua gave a fearless grin. "It looks like *they* plan to disperse these attack particles all over this stratum to eliminate my escape."

"A bad situation?"

"Does it look like it?"

Acqua muttered something under his breath, and the moisture in the air became his ally. He sensed the movements touching the moisture, getting a rough estimation of the Bowing Images' dispersal pattern.

Then he heard a soft sound of leaves scraping from nearby brush. He glanced over and saw a powered suit among the trees, its armor reflecting blue light. From a short distance away, he heard a different kind of start-up noise. They must have prepared short-term city armored police cars, making use of both gasoline engines and electric ones.

He wasn't smiling. "Testing the enemy's strength, are they? I'll introduce them to what I call my dirty mercenary style."

"I would prefer if you refrained from indiscreet bloodshed."

"I don't know for sure, but they're probably all unmanned. I don't sense human presences in them. That must have been how they got this close, but..."

Vroom!! A new sound split the air. It was the sound of Acqua pulling his especially large mace, over five meters long, from the shadows at his feet.

"Simply wonderful, isn't it? Academy City?" he said, heaving the metal lump onto his shoulder. "They went out of their way to make a battlefield where no blood had to be shed. How considerate. A perfect way to get used to things."

As if in response, the enemy group moved. In a corner of that nighttime park, several shadows surrounded him.

A volley of bullets flew. Bowing Images shot toward him, too small to be seen by the naked eye.

But Acqua didn't fall. He dodged the bullets and blew away the Images, sometimes borrowing their power to accurately deal with the bullets—which were flying in unnaturally twisting paths—and immediately shifting to a counterattack.

I don't know how the science works, but there must be someone in command here, hiding somewhere.

In a single breath, Acqua broke through their encirclement, his mace, over five meters long, stabbing into the side of an armored car like a spear. He ignored its weight, swinging the car itself around on his mace, crashing it into several powered suits. Then he swung the mace down toward the ground, causing the car caught on it to explode into a million pieces. Finally, after letting the Bowing Images floating in the air restrain him, by some spell, he walked calmly into the roiling flames.

I will tear off these powered suits' armor, wrench open the armored cars' chassis, and check every last one of them!!

Acqua of the Back, of God's Right Seat, worked.

While thunder and destruction dominated all.

3

Japan and England had a time difference of about nine hours. Right now, it was the middle of the night in Japan, but in London, it was still evening. Of course, because of their different latitudes, the English sun set earlier in the autumn and winter. The sky there was already growing purple.

The Royal Academy of Arts.

This museum of art, counted as one of the most prestigious in all

England, also sponsored art schools to foster the next generation of artists. And even at this hour, the voices of lecturers had yet to wane.

Standing on the platform as teacher, lit by fluorescent lighting, was Sherry Cromwell.

"We'll be discussing coats of arms today."

Her hair was yellow like a lion's, and her skin was the color of chocolate. Her clothing was a ragged, worn, black gothic lolita dress. Sherry was known as a talented sculptor, too, but her aesthetic didn't make sense in any works but her own…That, anyway, was her students' opinion of her.

"You know, coats of arms. The things with family crests on them. Not some strange, occult markings—though I suppose there are some of that variety, but that's getting off topic."

A few stifled laughs from the students. They must have thought she was joking. The sorcerer Sherry ignored them and moved on.

"What we call a coat of arms is actually a combination of several elements, but what I brought today is the one that goes in the center—the escutcheon." Her voice was drawling. "I'm sure those here aim to earn your daily bread by putting paintbrush to canvas, but when you want to impart a message to a work you create, this type of knowledge sometimes comes in handy. Anyway, it's a way of avoiding artist's block. Basically, just ignore everything your teacher is saying."

There came a reserved knock on the lecture room door. With the example escutcheon up on the platform, Sherry glanced dubiously that way.

The door opened slightly and without a sound, revealing a young office worker for this art school. She'd just arrived here this year. With a slight bend of her little head, she said, voice apologetic, "I'm sorry…There's someone calling you from the British Library…"

"Oh," said Sherry, her finger running along the heraldry's edge. She thought for a moment. "Guess you're on your own for a while, class," she said to her students with incredible flippancy, scratching her head and leaving the lecture room.

When she went into the hallway, the petite office worker looked at her nervously. "I'm, well, sorry about that."

"Don't worry about it," said Sherry. "They like self-study better anyway. You can't teach people how to make art. The ones who don't like self-study aren't cut out to be creators in the first place."

"I...I see..." The office worker smiled vaguely.

In a slightly annoyed voice, Sherry asked, "Anyway, someone called?"

"Oh, yes. They're on the phone now. Please come to the office."

The office worker led Sherry into the room. One of the telephones on a business desk was blinking, indicating a call on hold.

"That one?"

"Yes. It's the British Library...Are they asking about how to handle pieces of art?"

"Something like that."

The British Museum and St. George's Cathedral frequently contacted Sherry. The others in her life seemed to think the places were requesting appraisals or repairs on old pieces of art.

The office worker bowed to her, then went back to her own desk. Sherry tiredly picked up the phone.

An awfully relaxed female voice came over from the other end. *"Oh my. Am I correct in thinking that I'm speaking to Miss Sherry?"*

"...I just knew it would be you, Orsola. Christ. Don't they have any other book specialists around there?"

In response to Sherry's extremely fed-up tone, the woman named Orsola giggled. *"Well! You do know that bulk trash goes out on Mondays and Fridays."*

"I get it, I get it. You're rewinding your words. Just get to the point," said Sherry flatly, urging her on. She'd learned how to deal with the woman of late.

Orsola's story went like this.

"I've been doing some research into past accounts of magical incidents still in the British Library to find information on God's Right Seat and Acqua of the Back."

"Yeah, you told me before I left this morning. Find anything?"

"As a result of verifying things like eyewitness accounts of September thirtieth, the man in question, before taking on the name 'Acqua

of the Back,' was apparently a central figure in England. There are several first-hand testimonies of this."

"And you told me that this afternoon."

"There are also a few testimonies that state he was a knight of England."

"Huh?" Sherry frowned in thought for the first time. *Acqua of the Back, a Roman Orthodox follower, was a knight of England...?*

In modern-day England, the peerage of "knight" was a public decoration. It had nothing to do with family. The queen would confer the title directly on any who made important achievements for the country. Knighthood wasn't passed on to children or grandchildren, either. It was sort of like a national honor award.

But apart from that, a sizable faction called the Knights still existed behind the scenes in England. They took up swords to protect the royalty and the people, treating any who would threaten them as an enemy, and risked their lives to wipe them out. And, just like Far Eastern samurai, they were supposed to have vanished with the development of firearms.

"...To think a leader of another denomination would have once been one of our knights," said Sherry. "If that's true, we have a big problem on our hands. In the worst case, Academy City could put us through the ringer and say this Acqua of the Back incident was our responsibility."

"However, when I looked at the records of knight names preserved in Buckingham Palace, I didn't find anyone who matched Acqua of the Back's characteristics."

"Then your info was a false lead?" asked Sherry. Perhaps it was a case of a magic-using mercenary being mistaken for one.

"*Hmm,*" replied Orsola, seeming to ponder for a moment. "*It is true that I couldn't find him in the knight name records, but...*"

"Eh?"

"Anyone chosen as a knight prepares an escutcheon for their family, yes? I contacted a craftsman on the outskirts of London, and he had an order form for an escutcheon from an unknown person...They

used a pseudonym, but apparently, it was canceled part of the way through production."

"...I see." Sherry's lips curled. "A coat of arms' design encodes lineage, history, and role. You can investigate them to uncover the identity of this knight who isn't in the database."

"Yes...I decided there might be information to be gained from the illustrations. I sent the order form to you, with them, um, 'over fax.'"

Sherry looked at the fax machine just as it was spitting out paper. The young office worker from before ran over to it.

Sherry got the bundle from her, about ten pages in all, then spread the pages out on her desk. She ran her index finger over what was written. This was more like a machine blueprint than a piece of art. The pages were in monochrome and had color specifications written in all over, which really only served to deepen that impression.

"...Two main colors—blue for the base, with green to decorate. The animals being used...A dragon, a unicorn, and...Is this woman a selkie? The shield is divided in four, and if there are three animals to place on it, that means..."

"Does it tell you anything?"

Eventually, after gazing at the illustrations, Sherry sighed. "Something simple, yeah."

"I see."

"A dragon, a unicorn, and a selkie. All creatures that don't actually exist," explained Sherry. "The colors of the coat of arms are odd, too. You can't overlap a basic color like blue with another like green. It's against the rules...It's so indecent it makes me want to laugh. This guy must have been really unhappy about being placed on the list of Knights."

Like a phonograph, Sherry translated the information on the figures into words.

"I'm almost certain this person was welcomed by the royal faction and, unable to refuse, grudgingly accepted a summons to the knighting ceremony. Which means...he was a combat pro working as a freelancer before becoming a knight. And probably doing work that benefited England…For a lowly mercenary to be chosen as a knight indicates he followed through with his own upright moral code even on dirty battlefields. There's no more annoying enemy than one without any dirt on their record."

Just to be sure, she checked the date on the order form. It was from over ten years ago. The fact that a craftsman had been cherishing this order form, which was both old and supposedly canceled, gave her a glimpse of how much popularity Acqua of the Back had had during his days working for England.

"*Also,*" added Orsola, "*the requirements for being named a knight in the magic world state that only someone from England can receive it. Should I create a list of mercenaries stationed at bases in England?*"

"No," said Sherry, tapping on the animals drawn on the pages with her index finger. "A dragon, a unicorn, and a selkie. All three of these appear in legends across the entire United Kingdom, not just in England—in Scotland, Wales, and Northern Ireland, too."

"*…? I was under the impression that unicorns were from Greece.*"

"Elizabeth the First supposedly had a unicorn horn in her personal collection. Turned out it was just a regular animal bone, though," muttered Sherry. "In any case, this is someone born in the United Kingdom, a mercenary-for-hire working for England's benefit…This whole story of a lone-wolf merc who wasn't in any rigid sorcerer's society being welcomed as a knight is pretty suspicious. And given how they couldn't turn down a request they weren't happy with…Check anyone the royal faction treated with some importance."

4

The fifty members of Amakusa, Saiji Tatemiya first and foremost, were in a back alley in District 22's seventh stratum. Tatemiya had gotten a call; he was holding his phone in one hand while talking to his comrades.

"Looks like an unmanned Academy City mech unit ran into Acqua of the Back in a park on the third stratum."

That put everyone present on edge. The third stratum was where Kamijou and Itsuwa had just been attacked.

It went without saying who won the fight this time, as well. Acqua of the Back was a monster, and they knew beyond a doubt that a crowd of mass-produced machines wouldn't be enough to kill him.

Tatemiya looked at Ushibuka, who was nearby.

"...Are we going?" asked Ushibuka.

"No," said Tatemiya, shaking his head and clapping his phone closed. "We'd be going in blind. I think we all know how that would turn out. Let's wait for word from England. We need optimal preparation and an optimal strategy, then we'll challenge him to an optimal fight at an optimal time." He paused. "This is the final battle. This is what it means to get serious."

Acqua of the Back had floored Kamijou, their precious comrade and one who saved their lives, but though they knew his current location, they would endure for now. Hellish flames probably raged in Tatemiya's mind. But for the sake of a single victory, he stifled all those emotions—and told them that they would wait.

"Now isn't the optimal time. To make the best plan, we have time to wait for Miss Orsola's data organization skills. What does that leave us to do now? It's simple—we have to make optimal preparations."

Tatemiya looked around. The scattered members of Amakusa got to work cleaning and maintaining their swords, spears, and other weapons. To follow their principle of hiding and waiting, they normally had to give up a certain amount of weapon hardness or power, but now they were reinforcing them, removing their limiters.

"...Please, wait about three hours."

Suddenly, someone spoke. Tatemiya looked over and found Itsuwa, wearing a leather belt to tuck up her sleeve like the Shinsengumi. She was looking down as she reinforced her spear—actually, it was almost a full-fledged retrofit. Since her spear was made of several short sticks that attached to one another, it necessarily fell short on hardiness. Now, however, she was spraying a fixative on the length of the shaft, making the resin weapon a size thicker, while also using sandpaper to polish the surface to a smooth one.

"It will take a bit of time for me to get this into a state where I'm comfortable using it, and to sharpen the blade to use against that monster…Please leave it to me. He hit me directly with his attacks, so I know what kind of weapon I need to fight him skillfully…"

After using the sandpaper to reshape the spear, if there was a part of the resin that had gotten too thin, she sprayed it once again. She repeated that process several dozen times, again and again and again.

Scratch! Scratch!! Even the noise of her whittling the resin down sounded like it had bloodlust in it. Tatemiya felt a minor chill run down his spine. She was like a psycho killer, polishing her knife in the middle of the night. He thought, *Uh, crap. Did I get ahead of myself when I criticized her before?*

Nearby, Ushibuka must have been thinking the same thing. He whispered into Tatemiya's ear.

"(…What now? Now it's like you incited her too much and set a petrochemical complex on fire.)"

"(…W-well!! Listen here. She was acting like an empty shell or something in that hospital, so, well, yeah!! I was just cheering her up.)"

"(…You absolute idiot!! You *didn't* have any plan in mind when you incited her, did you?! Now we might have first-row seats to see how terrifying a girl in love can be!!)"

"(…What?! How is it *my* fault?! What do you think I should have done back there?!)"

"Tatemiya, Ushibuka?" murmured Itsuwa. Both the men shot upright at attention, unmoving. Itsuwa, still looking down, continued, her expression unreadable. "I'll be fine, all right? Could you please let me focus?"

Her face was blank, and her voice was incredibly level.

That was all she said, though, before going back to sanding down the side of her spear again. It was slowly evolving to be easier to carry, easier to use, and easier to kill.

Tatemiya and Ushibuka turned into shivering, stammering messes. Their comrades nearby sighed deeply at them.

Itsuwa seemed somehow awfully violent today, so Tatemiya secretly kept himself busy by using leather belts to tuck up his own sleeves, reinforcing his clothing with magic, and comparing notes with everyone else to make sure they had a firm grasp on the surrounding geography.

In the meantime, Tatemiya and Ushibuka, almost seriously, put their hands together in prayer for Acqua of the Back, who wasn't here right now.

You might have your own stuff going on, Acqua, but now that our Itsuwa is in a murderous rampage mode, you're on your own, buddy.

"(…I…I really, really, really don't want to be responsible for holding Itsuwa back when she snaps,)" said Tatemiya quietly.

"(…I—I—I concur,)" whispered Ushibuka.

Just then, Tatemiya's ringtone went off.

"Oh my. Would I happen to be speaking to Mr. Tatemiya?"

"Ack, Miss Orsola!! Your voice is a salve for the soul!!"

With something important in his mind about to give way, Tatemiya stood there, about to collapse into tears.

Orsola, though, didn't understand the situation. *"Um, if this is the wrong person, then I do apologize. I will hang up—"*

"Don't hang up!! If you do, I'll fall back into that sea of nervous tension!!"

Grasping at straws, Tatemiya fully engrossed himself into his conversation with Orsola. He switched his phone to speaker mode, so that everyone could hear, and waited for her to speak.

"I…I have new information regarding Acqua of the Back," she reported, unusually hesitant for someone who always went at her own pace. *"I've discovered his real name—William Orwell. He's a magic mercenary born in England, belonging to nobody. Of course, he wasn't a Roman Orthodox follower since birth; the record states that as a young boy, he was baptized in an English Puritan church. As a mercenary, he was always a lone wolf and appears to have specialized in bringing down enemy positions."*

Specialized in.

That implied bringing down positions wasn't all. In his many battles, the thing he'd been *best* at was point control. That didn't mean he couldn't do any other kinds of battle. If that was true, William Orwell would have lost long ago, and he wouldn't be here now.

"Also, William apparently has a sorcerer's name as well. He has engraved the name Flere210 into his mind."

"...Flere, huh...?"

Magic names used Latin words. *Flere*'s literal meaning was "tear," the droplet. They didn't know what meaning was behind that, though. Still, William Orwell had enough of a reason to name himself that—and the overwhelming ability to be able to.

A saint—that word, expressing an entirely different sort of existence than the rest of them, passed through the back of Tatemiya's mind. "What kind of record did William Orwell have during his mercenary days?"

"In western Russia, supporting the Astrologers' Brigade. In central France, the battle to annihilate the Knights of Orleans. Near the Dover Strait, the battle to rescue the third princess of England...There are too many to count."

Participating in many battles, gaining victory, and returning alive—that, by itself, spoke to Acqua of the Back's massive abilities. As Orsola listed off the names of the battles Acqua took part in, Tatemiya recognized several of them. All were known as heated conflicts. Battlefields they could praise only as nightmares, the sort even Amakusa all together couldn't overcome.

"He's a tough opponent...Actually, he sounds almost invincible."

"However, William Orwell does not seem to have been the sort to resolve all problems before him with violence. For example, he went to one war-torn region with few medical facilities and passed on medicinal knowledge to decrease death rates, went to a starving village and taught them how to prepare burdock root as food since it wasn't being used for it in that region...He evidently did much outside of fighting. Some people apparently called him a sage."

That was only something he could have done if he understood the reality of war. Some problems couldn't be solved just by sending in a large force or donating money. It took the feel of the battlefield's air on your skin, an understanding of what the people there needed, and an assurance that they could do what you did, too. Only that would create a permanent, not a temporary, increase in their quality of life. It would appear that Acqua of the Back wasn't a mere battle idiot after all.

He was an intelligent beast, with a tenacious body and a flexible mind.

"*I cannot find anything one could call a weakness*," said Orsola. "*It appears he has been using his meteoric powers as a saint ever since he was a freelance mercenary.*

"*...And on top of that, he wields power as a member of God's Right Seat after converting to the Roman Orthodox Church.*"

That meant all those legends from his mercenary days were built back before William Orwell even became Acqua of the Back. His abilities were beyond that now. And it wasn't just additional strength he had—he'd gained an entirely new game board to battle on. Once again, Tatemiya was astounded at how great this enemy they'd made was. He was probably more terrifying than their own Priestess baring her fangs.

How on earth does he control all that power?

If you looked at Kanzaki, it would seem like she was naturally controlling her powers as a saint. But it wasn't actually that easy. If a normal sorcerer like Tatemiya tried to handle it, it would be so much he'd destroy himself instantly.

And Acqua commanded even more than she did.

...Means he's probably stronger in magical ability, too.

"*The plan was for England to knight William, but a week before the ceremony, he vanished. An in-progress escutcheon was thus left sitting in a craftsman's house.*"

And when he next appeared, he was an enemy of England. It was a mystery what happened in that time, but that wasn't important right now.

"I don't expect you to find any weaknesses. Don't you at least know how Acqua fights? Like what weapons he uses or what combat style?"

"His combat style is completely self-taught. He appears to call it 'dirty mercenary style.' In terms of his weapons, he uses a steel mace over five meters in length. This says it outwardly looks like a knight's lance."

Tatemiya and the others already knew that; they'd fought him directly.

"Also...The way he moves during battle is unique. Instead of running, he appears to slide over the surface of the ground."

"...?" They hadn't given that a thought. Was that why they hadn't heard him approaching? Now that he considered it, she was probably right. Still, Acqua moved so fast that aside from changing direction, it pretty much looked like he just disappeared.

"It seems to be a movement spell that uses water somehow. Cars slip on ice because of the thin layer of water between the ice and the wheels, right?"

"Which means...He's been good at using water even before they called him Acqua of the Back..."

Vento of the Front, Terra of the Left, Acqua of the Back. If they were each associated with one of the four archangels, that meant Acqua's territory was Gabriel, God's "power"—whose attribute was water. He hadn't used any special attacks, any water spells, during their fight, probably because he thought them beneath it.

...All right. How do we plan for that, exactly?

There were too many unknowns, values whose upper limit was too high for them to even imagine. It made Tatemiya want to laugh.

Then it happened.

"Whatever our enemy, there's only one thing we have to do..."

Quietly.

Itsuwa, who had been reinforcing her spear, murmured, her lips barely moving at all:

"Isn't that right, Tatemiya?"

The words *you better not run away* were hidden in there, and Tatemiya's hand with the cell phone in it started to tremble.

5

Three AM.

Acqua of the Back lingered on a bridge in School District 22's third stratum.

During his route from the park to here, he'd felled eight self-propelled Bowing Image control antennae, seventeen armored cars, and thirty-eight powered suits. All were unmanned. He would defeat one enemy, move, encounter more there, wipe them out, repeat…But he still couldn't find who was taking command, controlling the operation. His opponent must have been using their head more than Acqua gave them credit for.

Without a glance to the artificial night sky projected by the planetarium canopy overhead, he found himself thinking, *Vento's divine judgment would have made this easy…*

Still, it hadn't even been an hour yet, and the enemy had withdrawn. It was such a one-sided defeat that the Academy City leaders must have decided the battle a waste of military resources. Acqua agreed. He shuddered to think how much capital had gone into manufacturing those metal trash heaps. People poured insane amounts of money into modern weapons—so much the numbers stopped making sense. He thought they would be better off finding a more economical use for it all.

"…But surprisingly, they don't seem to be idiots."

That was his evaluation of their skillful withdrawal. You could say it about any field: Professionals had a lot of pride in their own work. For someone in the service, that was straight power. The thrashing he'd given them would make everyone talk. Their withdrawal meant Academy City had a leader who had pushed that aside, used enough logical arguments to force the others to understand the actual situation, and urged a swift retreat.

Of course, it didn't matter how excellent that leader's political skills were, nor how much strength and brawn they commanded. It didn't change what Acqua had to do.

Destroy the Imagine Breaker.

...And intercept all elements who would block him.

Now, then. Acqua took out a pocket watch and checked the time. *Still nineteen hours left until the negotiated time is up...*

He closed the watch, put it back in his pants pocket, then looked to the side using only his eyes.

"Come to a conclusion?" said Acqua into the darkness. "You have half a day until the time limit. Have you made the preparations already?"

From out of the dark came a scrape...of footsteps.

More than one set. Around fifty of them in all. All of them members of the Amakusa-Style Crossist Church, known as a branch of English Puritanism. Their footsteps, surrounding him, were three-dimensional, meaning that they had all appeared, as though seeping out, from every nook and cranny in the metal bars making up the bridge.

There were men, women, children, and adults, and all of them wore normal clothing you could find anywhere. But their hands gripped swords, spears, axes, bows, whips, and other weapons, all ominously reflecting the streetlights. Among them were weapons that even Acqua, as a mercenary, hadn't seen before—a *kusarigama* and a *jitte*, characteristic of the East—and even one that looked like a flute made of metal.

At the front stood the Amakusa-Style Crossist Church's vicar pope, Saiji Tatemiya.

There was a simple reason he knew his name: He'd heard it muttered during the previous battle, called among allies and when changing tactics. Intelligence gathering on the battlefield was another necessary skill for a mercenary.

"Well, I mean, you gave us an impossible problem," said Tatemiya. "Means we don't have to worry about it, so we came to a quick decision. Guess I have you to thank for that, at least."

Tatemiya held a large sword, a flamberge. Like claymores and other two-handed swords, it had been made extra-large for crushing both thick armor and the enemy inside.

His weapon was enormous, 180 centimeters in length. But from Acqua's viewpoint, it still looked no longer than a child's stick.

"An impossible problem?" he repeated, smiling as he tapped his foot on the ground. Without a sound, his shadow wriggled, and out came a lump of metal over five meters long. "You stand against the Roman Orthodox Church's two billion, and yet I said you'd get out of it with a mere arm. I would think this a bargain."

"The Roman Church isn't our enemy. It's people like you—the ones making the normal God-fearing people dance for you, preying on them."

"Hmm. Does this mean our negotiations have failed?"

"What else could it possibly mean?"

"Nothing, I suppose. It's not for me to worry about. You're the ones who should be worrying—because you've abandoned the only possibility you had of living through this."

Acqua reaffirmed his grip on the gigantic mace stretching from the shadow under him, then gave it a light swing with his wrist, as though flicking a tennis racket.

"I'll say this once more to be certain," he said. "I am a saint."

"..."

"And I also have power as part of God's Right Seat."

"..."

"If you've properly understood that, and still say you will risk your lives to fight and protect someone, then I look forward to it—the possibilities of man, or what have you. I look forward to your vaunting being more than nonsense. I'm sure you've poured every bit of your strength into tricks and aces. I will accept every last one of them."

Acqua changed.

Not in a visible way. He didn't sprout angel wings or a halo overhead, or anything concrete like that. However, something unseen had spouted from his whole body.

"And I will still win."

With a rumble, Acqua took just half a step forward.

He didn't do it to move but to prepare his metal mace. It was a quiet, grave, decisive motion to display his resolve and determination to crush every last one of those he saw as enemies.

"I will prove that battles are not decided by good or evil, but by strength and weakness. I pray that you will draw out at least one of my own trump cards. If you cannot even reach that point, then I will grant you not the title of weak, but that of fools—"

Acqua didn't continue after that.

Ga-bam!!

Itsuwa, having lost her patience, ignored their conversation and struck suddenly, her full intent behind it.

The Friulian spear she'd stabbed wordlessly shot toward Acqua in a line, as fast as a flash of lightning. Immediately, she activated a spell on its tip, one she'd built using the cold night air—and detonated it. *Boom!!* Flashes of light scattered while bursts of wind whipped about, mercilessly smashing everything to pieces—not just Acqua, who had taken the hit directly, but the asphalt nearby.

It even flipped over her own ally, Saiji Tatemiya.

"I-Itsuwa…Hello…?" he said softly, shocked, but Itsuwa didn't turn around. He just got an electric feeling coming off her shoulders.

She glared into the billowing dust, keeping her spear ready, and clicked her tongue. A mace tore through the curtain of gray, revealing an unharmed Acqua.

"Do you not think it polite to listen until the end?"

"…If you want to talk, I'll listen later." Itsuwa, far from growing nervous, actually took another step in. "*After* I've beaten the living, standing, walking, talking, breathing shit out of you! If your jaw is still in good enough condition to talk anyway!!"

Itsuwa's shouts could pierce eardrums, and though her face was expressionless, a strange power was gathering in the middle of her brow. The Amakusa members, with pained looks, variously put hands to their heads and looked away.

"(…Bad, bad, bad!! Itsuwa's gone off the deep end!!)"

"(…It's your fault! You were careless and told her at the hospital to prove she was the best woman out there, and now her feminine heart is at full power!!)"

"(...Idiot. A woman in love would make even God an enemy.)"

As the men chattered to each other quietly, Tsushima gave them an oddly cool reprimand.

Itsuwa and Acqua ignored their exchanges, facing each other down. At some point, Amakusa's central point had changed completely.

"Hmm. That's very heroic of you, but I'd rather you show me actual power to match your words."

"Please, don't worry. Even if we end up pieces of flesh, we will rip and tear and cut and hack and shred you to bits so that you regret what you've done!!"

A voice came from behind her, crying out, "What?! I didn't think we were going that far!!" She ignored it and took another step forward.

The two of them had come into definite striking range. Leaving behind Saiji Tatemiya as he watched in bafflement, they clashed.

6

Explosions ripped through the late-night air on the bridge.

The difference in speed between Acqua, who wielded the immense powers of a saint, and Itsuwa, just a regular person, was vast. Acqua lurched straight for her so quickly that he disappeared from the human eye. All his muscle mass expanded at once, and he whipped his giant mace like a guillotine.

Itsuwa barely managed to move her spear a half step later. She took a stance with it along the path of Acqua's attack, meaning to stop it. But Acqua had no attacks that could be stopped.

However...

"!!"

With a *grrrrrieeek* like two boulders colliding, Itsuwa's spear stopped Acqua's mace.

Normally, a mere Friulian spear would have been blown to smithereens, along with Itsuwa's slight body.

"That spear..."

"Yes—it's coated in fifteen hundred layers of resin." Itsuwa grinned, barely holding her weapon in place. "It represents the rings indicating wood's age, and the hidden form's identity is the reproductive power of plant life. Until this spell reaches its limit, this hardness will only continue to grow firmer with the passage of time. Every second that goes by makes it sturdier. Have a taste, and know the power of my Weeds!!"

"However, you have several other spells layered on it..."

"...Why was clothing adopted in every civilization in the world? Do you need an explanation on what hidden forms are for?"

The sweater Itsuwa wore was unnaturally torn near the armpit, revealing pale skin beneath. Almost as though she had substituted it to take the mace's damage for her.

"To defend the wearer, yes...This must be its most important meaning. However, it is an ancillary damage-reduction spell, not convenient enough to defend against any sort of attack unarmed."

Acqua hadn't seen anything like this in the last battle. And they didn't have to be stingy about it now. In other words, Amakusa's members had been very quick to get such highly effective Soul Arms and spells ready.

But that wasn't what surprised him the most.

She kept up with my speed...?

He was a saint. His speed was overwhelming. No normal human could keep up with it. Itsuwa should have been dead right now, unable to move a finger.

And yet she'd reacted.

She'd only had half a step to catch up later; she didn't have any time to switch to a counterattack. And yet her defense had still worked.

How? Acqua wondered, but then he realized the answer a moment later:

There was a certain regularity to the fifty Amakusa members' movements. A more unique regularity than a simple, efficient battle line. As soon as he thought Itsuwa was their center, the center moved. When he looked for it again, he would find it scattered among all of them; it wasn't an actual center. But the moment he took his mind off that center, it would return to Itsuwa. It was an odd sensation, this center, almost like a creature sliding through the single group.

Sometimes it would coalesce, other times it would scatter, and like the sand in an hourglass, it combined their individual movements into one larger meaning.

Are they reinforcing one another's kinetic vision and physical abilities?

"Parlor tricks...," he said with a frown at their movements—which seemed *accustomed to fighting against saints.* Sainthood was a rare talent that less than twenty people in the world had. Only so many people would personally see one in their lifetime.

Hmph. I see. The Amakusa-Style Crossist Church. A saint like myself was once a member of their ranks.

With that taken into consideration, their eyes must have been used to the speed, strength, and intelligence of a saint. And they had the brains to bring out that experience, resulting in her having made a spell to keep up with Acqua.

He pulled his mace back once, then readied it again, giving Itsuwa another look. "But it's still too slow."

"?!"

Sshwohhh!! The saint charged in again.

Before Itsuwa could feel the blast of wind, the mace came at her in a horizontal sweep. She barely caught it, but by the time her clothing had ripped and allowed her to magically elude the impact, the next attack was already coming from overhead. She tried to swing her spear at it, but that was when the first strike's impact washed over her, sending her body falling backward.

As Acqua's second attack fell more swiftly at her than the shock from the first, the middle-aged Isahaya sacrificed his katana to delay the mace's path for a half second, and in that time, the woman Tsushima grabbed Itsuwa by the neck and hurled her aside.

The third attack Acqua performed passed through the spot Itsuwa had just occupied, mercilessly crushing the asphalt on the bridge.

Go-gong!! The bridge itself swayed, unstable.

Though Isahaya had avoided a direct hit, the barrage of asphalt fragments pelted his body, sending him flying.

Acqua tried to pursue Itsuwa further, but then he saw a glare of light mixed into the gray dust.

A wire.

No—more than one.

The next thing he knew, all those people, close to fifty, with the spear-wielder at the center, had launched ultra-thin wires from their fingertips. Each of them controlled seven strands. Three hundred fifty wires in all formed a spider's web, attacking Acqua from all directions.

"Hmph."

Acqua didn't dodge.

Ga-pah!! He exposed himself to the ultra-thin blades slicing through the air and then, on top of that, used a strength technique to force them all to rip.

It was far from a certain-kill move—it had stopped him for less than a second.

Acqua of the Back, of God's Right Seat, had just displayed his overwhelming power.

"You killed me."

Quietly.

A voice, whispering into his ear:

"YOU KILLED ME."

I see, so that's it...?! The same moment Acqua clenched his teeth, a red mist-like gas spurted from the severed wires. It expanded so far it was like it had bleached out the black night sky, immediately beginning to engulf his body.

"...The hidden form—Punishment for Murderers."

Itsuwa's mutter came to him from where she stood, in the center of the broken bridge. The red mist suddenly inflated from within, bursting.

Amakusa's sorcery had whipped up a massive explosion from within the mist. Not only had it trapped him in an inescapable prison—now an overwhelming explosion danced through the inside. No matter how fast he was, he wouldn't escape it.

"This spell redefines the wires as individual lifelines, then delivers punishment on any who destroy them. It uses religious views shared throughout the world, east and west, in every culture—it holds the meaning of negative resentment, which no civilization's defensive techniques can block."

The mass of red consuming Acqua burst a second time, then a third. *Boom!! Bam!!* Dull sounds, one after another, like explosions occurring underwater. They chained further, multiplying, until the red mist hung like a twisted bunch of grapes.

The most advanced technique they had, unachievable with one's power alone, created by the singular entity known as Amakusa.

But the looks on their faces were not bright.

Da-boom!!

Their killing spell tore open from within, then scattered in every direction.

What caused it was a far more powerful explosion than the ones Amakusa had prepared. The blast was a rank stronger than the one they'd brought to kill a man, and it easily destroyed the prison.

As dust swirled into water vapor, a gray curtain fell across their surroundings.

From beyond it came a deep male voice.

"I will tell you of my sacrifice."

An enormous silhouette wavered behind that curtain. Something circulated there, something like a core within the shadow.

"My characteristics are of Gabriel. And because of his connection to the Annunciation, I can, to some extent, use a technique related to the Virgin Mother—a secret ritual known as the Adoration of Mary."

His words alone continued on.

"The Adoration of Mary attenuates severe punishment."

Acqua of the Back, of God's Right Seat.

His voice alone dominated the world.

"Those who believe will be saved. But one of Jesus's characteristics is to levy severe, suitable punishment on those who do not follow his rules. The Adoration of Mary mitigates this. Like a substitute for a woman who runs away from a convent, one who will take her space in the rolls until the woman's return."

The silhouette slowly moved.

Forward, to break the curtain made of dust and vapor.

"Unlike the Son of God, born at once as man, as God, and as the Holy Spirit, Mary is pure child of man alone, a rare being who has stepped deeply into God's realm. It is said she received from this the role of intervening with God on the behalf of those suffering severe punishments despite having incredibly pure hearts."

His voice rumbled.

High and mighty, and unconcealed.

"The conclusion is this. My special quality is the Mercy of Mary, which nullifies punishment. It can warp even the impartial and definite Last Judgment. It can change even the signposts sending the souls of the dead to heaven or hell. All acts of restriction based on severe punishment versus sin and evil have no meaning for me. To wipe away the sin of murder, I don't even need to move a finger. Did you honestly think this would work against one who can erase even the sins of God hi—?"

Da-bam!! Another explosion. The gray curtain covering Acqua was swept away, all in an instant.

"Hmm. Do they not think it polite to listen until the end?"

Acqua put his giant mace on his shoulder and sighed in annoyance. Nobody was here but him. They'd kindly left him a spell that would leave only the sense of their presence behind. All fifty of the Amakusa combat personnel had disappeared into thin air.

He was the only one left on the bridge, but he grinned like a hunter trailing the footmarks of his prey.

"I suppose this makes the pursuit more enjoyable."

7

The current members of Amakusa, centered around Saiji Tatemiya, had moved to a small plaza about three hundred meters from the bridge. They had acted alongside the spell they'd placed on Acqua, Taboo Against Murder; they'd put the spell together beforehand so that they could quickly flee if it was broken.

Someone with his skill would surely sense their presence and mana flow. There were only so many places in this underground city to hide, and Amakusa had a good reason they couldn't flee anyway.

"He broke it, as we thought. What now, Vicar Pope?" asked Ushibuka, collecting the wires, cut apart like strands of cotton.

"...Would have been nice if it got him, but things won't be so easy."

Tatemiya, flamberge still in hand, looked around. Amakusa had displayed enough physical ability to keep up with Acqua of the Back, but it wasn't actually that convenient a thing. Besides, if all fifty of them could move with the same speed as a saint at all times, they'd be more treasured than the saints were.

"Deception will only get us so far," Itsuwa huffed, trying to catch her breath.

The physical enhancement spell had actually been keyed by touching someone's back. The hidden ritual was "physical recovery by touching the back." While fighting, they constantly changed their formation, touching one another's backs when moving or crossing. It restored their physical abilities and enhanced them temporarily.

The spell couldn't be used alone; as it benefited allies, it was unique to groups. In addition, when in an area with suitable "lines" for geomantic sleeping places and rest places, the effects were amplified.

They'd successfully kept up even with the saint by heightening their allies' physical abilities over and over, but they couldn't completely repel the enemy's attacks. And if the formation itself was thrown into disarray, they wouldn't be able to strengthen one another.

This wasn't enough to defeat Acqua of the Back.

That was the kind of monster a saint was.

"Which means we're going to have to use our trump card. We'll counterattack starting with Itsuwa, with her spear, following the form of the Son of God's execution. No holding back. Be ready for this."

Tatemiya looked around, particularly at Itsuwa, for confirmation.

Her Friulian spear still in both hands, the young woman nodded slightly.

That was when it happened:

Zzwahhh!! A chill crawled over the skin of everyone there. Some sort of giant presence was tearing through the dark, swiftly approaching them. They could feel it. No need to ask who it was—who could it have been but Acqua?

Amakusa still had its "trump card" plan. But because it was their big move, they couldn't use it right off the bat.

"Damn. Form up!!" shouted Tatemiya.

Amakusa's members moved like a wave. Not forward, backward, left, or right—but below. They got their hands into the artificial, tiled ground and wrenched open a one-meter-square section of tile as though it were a hatch. Underneath the surface waited a space of steel and concrete.

A damp metal staircase and railing, and thick, crisscrossing pipes. As the machinery made low, regular rumbles, Itsuwa pressed her back to the pipes in order to slip through the cracks available. This must have been a hydraulic generator and its transformer.

The partition between the underground city's strata was about ten meters thick. It seemed they were using the space for energy production facilities.

As Tatemiya, Itsuwa, and the others passed through the intricate passages, they set up the wires all over as traps. They didn't think they'd defeat Acqua with them. They just needed to buy time.

Amakusa continued, aiming ever lower.

For now, they would retreat from the third stratum, where Acqua was, to the unharmed fourth stratum to buy time. Then they'd make the necessary preparations for their trump card.

"You've shown me something good. Allow me to show you something better."

But suddenly, the deep male voice rang through the dimly lit space. It bounced many times, making it impossible to locate the source.

"I have the property of Gabriel. Surely you know what I can control."

"?!"

There was no time to react. The thick pipes crisscrossing through the concrete space promptly exploded from within. The water-carrying pipes were over one meter across and five centimeters thick—yet they tore apart like paper, sending a rain of guitar pick–sized metal fragments scattering. *Snap! Crack!!* Orange sparks burst this way and that. The speeding fragments were hitting the concrete and ricocheting.

"I can easily control the volume of water. Used the right way, I can make it into a bomb."

Ga-bam-bam-bam-bam!! The pipes exploded in all directions, one after another.

The cloud of metal fragments, pushed by the mixture of water and vapor, turned into a shotgun deluge that pelted the Amakusa. Itsuwa, finally reacting, knocked one fragment heading toward her face out of the air with her spear, but it instead threatened to mow her down completely.

The sheer force behind it was incredible, but something else bothered Itsuwa. A moment before the pipes ruptured, she'd seen what looked like shining letters. They spelled *laguz*.

A symbolic word.

"Wait...A water rune?!"

It was an incredibly commonplace sorcery, one that could even be called "a typical example of magic" due to how basic it was.

"That reaction...You must have learned something about God's Right Seat from Terra's corpse."

According to the English Puritan Church's report, because the bodies of those in God's Right Seat more closely resembled angels than humans and although they could use special spells, they weren't supposed to be able to use spells regular sorcerers could. So why?

"Is it truly that surprising? No, a member of God's Right Seat cannot use the normal magics of man. However, my Adoration of Mary spell effectively removes those promises, those bindings, those conditions."

He could use both the power of a saint and God's Right Seat...

And on top of that, he had a perfect grasp of both human and angelic spells.

"Did you not think it strange? When I first attacked, *who do you think used one of the most popular sorceries of all, Opila, to ward everyone off*?"

There was a vast difference in both attack varieties and power.

The monster was equipped with quality as well as quantity. He spoke only the truth, with no needless emotion expressed.

"Do not put me, Acqua of the Back, on the same level as those others from God's Right Seat."

Ugh...! Several more pipes ruptured, and finally, the turbine itself used to generate water power exploded, attacking her. Seeing the turbine's propeller whirling toward her like a rotary knife, Itsuwa went over the metal railing without using the stairs, falling straight down into the dark. She used her spear to pierce through a hatch in the floor, then leaned outside to see the ceiling section of the fourth stratum, the one right below the third.

From the floor where she was, it was about a twenty-meter drop. Along the ceiling were thin, metal walkways and crisscrossing stairs. The sight looked like a theater stage, and directly below her were not the buildings and roads of the fourth stratum but the giant planetarium screen, still displaying the surface sky. The giant sheet of fabric covering the city was hung from the ceiling with countless thin support beams and wires placed at regular intervals.

But Itsuwa didn't have the time to be rapt over the bizarre sight.

"...!! Where's Ac—?"

"I'm right here."

By the time she heard the voice suddenly next to her, she'd already felt wind pressure. Before she could turn that way, her spear moved out of reflex. It caught the weighty attack coming at her—but it immediately sent her careening fifteen meters away. He'd struck her down along with her spear.

Gshahh!! A dull sound followed, ringing in her ears.

Itsuwa, somehow enduring the damage to her whole body, tried to set herself up to land. But there was no footing. With no options left, she fell toward the giant screen.

Surprisingly, the screen supported her body without ripping. It must have also been engineered to prevent things from falling from the ceiling.

Not thinking about the unstable, sinking footing, Itsuwa readied her spear again and looked forward.

Acqua of the Back.

The man, carrying the mace on his shoulder, which was incomparably larger than her spear, jumped down from the railing himself, landing atop the screen.

"Let us leave the warm-up at that," he said quietly, angling his mace at her again. "We both hold weapons now. There is no reason they should not cross."

"...You're right," said Itsuwa slowly, pointing her spear's cross-shaped tip at Acqua. "But I can't guarantee I'm alone."

As soon as she said that, ceiling hatches over Acqua began popping open.

The members of Amakusa appeared from them. Every one was wounded, red staining different spots on their clothing, but their numbers hadn't yet decreased.

All fifty of them—one hundred eyes—focused on Acqua.

The monster, however, wasn't even scared.
"It matters not."
He swayed.
He didn't take a single step; his center of gravity alone had fallen.
"Come," he said as all the members of Amakusa dove for him.

8

Itsuwa charged Acqua directly. Before the man—who stood on the giant screen projecting a starry sky—responded, blades challenged him from the Amakusa men: from the left, right, back, and overhead.

Close to twenty sharp edges aimed for Acqua's body. Even if he dealt with those, thirty more would attack him after that.

An absolute number. No normal person could have dealt with even the first wave.

But Acqua responded.

Vwohh!! The giant mace split through the air. It batted away Ushibuka and Kouyagi, floating in midair, and the shock wave he'd purposely scattered to their surroundings assailed other ones. Ignoring the people in front of him who had been blown away or broken, Acqua slammed his mace straight behind him without looking.

His chain of movements was practically an explosion.

With Acqua at the center of the maelstrom, the skilled warriors fired away in every direction.

"!!"

Itsuwa, a moment away from adding her own attack to the mix, abruptly stopped herself on the screen.

Acqua used the chance to slide toward her as though skating across the floor.

Itsuwa immediately put up her guard, but he slipped through her defensive net, bringing his raised mace down toward her skull.

It was a flash of steel lightning.

But the strike didn't hit her.

Acqua felt the sensation of his attack whiffing. Itsuwa, who had just been in range, had disappeared. He looked and saw only the brightly colored sweater she'd been wearing clinging to the tip of the mace. His gaze moved from his hands to what was in front of him. Itsuwa stood a short distance away, wearing her tank top, which she'd somehow kept on despite shedding her sweater.

Acqua flicked the mace to remove the cloth scrap from it. "A substitute?"

"Unfortunately, I don't have very many of them," said Itsuwa quietly, readying her cross spear again. "Don't make me do something *too* embarrassing, please."

Before she finished speaking, they clashed again.

Acqua's mace, which looked like it could easily break the earth itself, came again.

But Itsuwa's spear responded. She must have reinforced her body with several spells, putting in tremendous effort to keep up with his sainted movements. He struck once, twice, then a third time. Itsuwa's motions were half a tempo slower, barely managing to deflect his attacks.

"You move well," said Acqua in honest praise of his enemy as he quickly swung the mace. "But can you keep this up? Your rhythm is steadily lowering."

"Urgh…!!"

Little by little, she was being pushed back as their gap widened. Once it passed a certain point, Itsuwa wouldn't be able to stop his strikes, and she'd be smashed to little bits.

In order to support her, other members of Amakusa, like Tsushima and Isahaya, attacked Acqua from several different directions, but his mace struck out with terrifying speed, acting like a wall to prevent their strikes. As he crossed blades with Itsuwa, Acqua controlled the combatants around him as though they were a mere distraction. And when he had the chance, he shone runic letters, counterattacking with highly pressurized water jets.

Tatemiya, dealing with the ferocity, glanced toward Itsuwa. "(…How's it coming?!)" he whispered through his teeth.

"(…I don't…have time…!!)"

"Itsu—!!" began Tatemiya in a shout, meaning to reposition the Amakusa members, but Acqua's attack came.

It knocked away his flamberge, which he'd abruptly gotten ready, and the shock wave sent him spinning into the giant screen.

"Let's see," said Acqua, getting his mace ready again as he watched Itsuwa's ragged breathing. "I shall enjoy seeing how many seconds you last." As he spoke, his muscles expanded all at once.

It was impossible to escape his range. His giant mace and Itsuwa's spear collided. She'd barely avoided a direct hit, but that was Itsuwa's limit. *Bam-bam-bam-bam-bam!!* Each time their weapons clashed—almost as though the cogs forming her attacks were sliding out of place—Itsuwa's speed clearly dropped more.

She didn't have room to counterattack. She couldn't even fully receive his attacks, which pounded the screen underfoot with shock waves. The special fabric, which must have had bulletproof fiber woven in or something, began to tear apart like stockings.

This was a hellish battle of attrition. A marathon. A race where a blender to grind human flesh was slowly approaching from behind the runners.

If she stopped, she was dead.

But if she kept running, she would go past her limits and destroy her own body.

The collision of weapons, bladed and blunt, was all that continued.

"Hnn...!!" Acqua sucked in a breath, and when he lifted his leg for another powerful step toward her, Itsuwa moved.

She didn't go forward, but backward. As hard as she could—to evade Acqua's attack.

It was a little retreat, only a few meters. From Acqua's perspective as someone with the physical abilities of a saint, it was a distance he could cross in a heartbeat. But for Itsuwa, this was a desperate decision. Because she'd jumped back with all her strength, she lost her balance and was about to topple over.

The young warrior couldn't engage him with another attack. Nor could she dodge one of his or defend it.

"Hmph," sniffed Acqua, moving to finish her off.

He dove into certain-kill range with the speed of a jet fighter carving through the air.

Zzzt!

But then he stopped—as though something had sewn him down.

"What…?"

Surprised, Acqua looked at his feet. His speedy movements were something he'd supported with a spell. By laying a thin film of water between his shoes and the ground, he could slide across it using the same logic as when tires slipped on ice.

The spell had failed without him realizing it.

Itsuwa shouldn't have had the leeway to invert his spell and destroy it. In fact, she'd made no motions to actually cast such a spell.

However…

Before he realized it, a faint light appeared. It came from his feet. An incomprehensible pattern extended from them, blocking the movement spell he'd been using.

The strike Itsuwa had failed to receive. The aftermath from it was a shock wave that had torn the screen underfoot. And the pattern of that torn fabric itself had constructed a circular shape, which, by curious coincidence, had blocked his movement spell.

Except—this was no coincidence.

The Amakusa-Style Crossist Church didn't use any special incantations or Soul Arms when they used sorcery. They constructed their spells by recovering and reassembling the magical symbols hidden in omnipresent, everyday items and events.

And above all…

Seeing how she'd gotten just a moment's opening from Acqua…

…Itsuwa, in front of him, had a very faint grin on her face.

As Acqua tipped forward, Itsuwa thrust her spear at him without mercy. Finally able to counterattack after everything, she struck with lightning speed.

Roar!! The straight strike tore through the air, and for the first time, Acqua took evasive action.

"Urgh?!" Acqua jumped not forward, back, left, or right, but up. The unstable screen at his feet didn't matter. With just one hop, he dove upward almost five meters, then hung by his foot, which he hooked onto one of the thin support beams holding up the screen.

"Tatemiya, everyone!!" And yet Itsuwa remained in her stance. She lowered herself, then once again thrust her Friulian spearhead at Acqua. "Time for the trump card!!"

After she called their names and mustered all her strength, the members of Amakusa, scattered about nearby, acted in concert. Some approached Itsuwa, while others took a certain set distance from her, reinforcing the formation that placed her as the central point.

Having caught one foot on the thin beam as he looked for a place to land, Acqua looked at the scene below and felt it—a focusing of all their wills and mana onto Itsuwa.

It was a warning. The first wave before something enormous happened.

Here it comes...!!

Before Acqua could speak, Itsuwa moved.

Ga-bam!! A burst of air.

By the time he perceived it as the sound of a human foot kicking away from the screen, Itsuwa had already shot through the night air with the force of a rocket or a space shuttle. The mind-boggling force caused several of the beams supporting the massive screen to break and collapse. In her hand, as she accelerated at a tremendous speed, was a small cloth that looked like a hand towel. She'd used it, tying it around the spear's shaft, to change her stance.

"A pipe spear?!"

By reducing the friction between her palm and the spear, she added speed and power to the shaft as it thrust. But Itsuwa was currently going for something different with the addition.

"Take this!"

And that was because, with the strike she was about to unleash, without any protection, she'd lose her hand at the wrist in the middle of the spell.

"Saintbreaker!!"

Ga-bam!! The spear exploded in Itsuwa's hands.

It wasn't a metaphor, or anything of the sort—it actually turned into a flash of light. This time, the straight, sharp thrust dug brutally into the middle of Acqua's gut. Pale blue lightning erupted from his back, cleaving the darkness of the night. Because of the terrible friction, the cloth wrapped around the shaft she gripped gave a puff of black smoke and blew away.

With a thunderous roar, a cross of light, different from the sparks erupting from Acqua's back, exploded out in four directions.

"…!!"

Before Acqua could manage to say anything, the hidden spell activated.

Itsuwa—no, the entirety of the Amakusa-Style Crossist Church—had just unleashed a literal Saintbreaker.

Because saints possessed similar physical characteristics to the Son of God, they, by idol worship theory, possessed the same type of talents and powers as Jesus.

On the other hand, by using artificial means to destroy the balance of those physical characteristics similar to Jesus, it was possible to temporarily seal away his powers as a saint.

Having abruptly lost that balance, the saint wouldn't merely lose their power—they'd be unable to control the power remaining inside them, be caught up in a runaway reaction, and be unable to move.

Once…

The Amakusa-Style Crossist Church had lost a saint.

A kind saint, who had left her home for fear of involving others with her strength. The members of Amakusa hadn't even had the strength to stop her.

After that, they had made a vow.

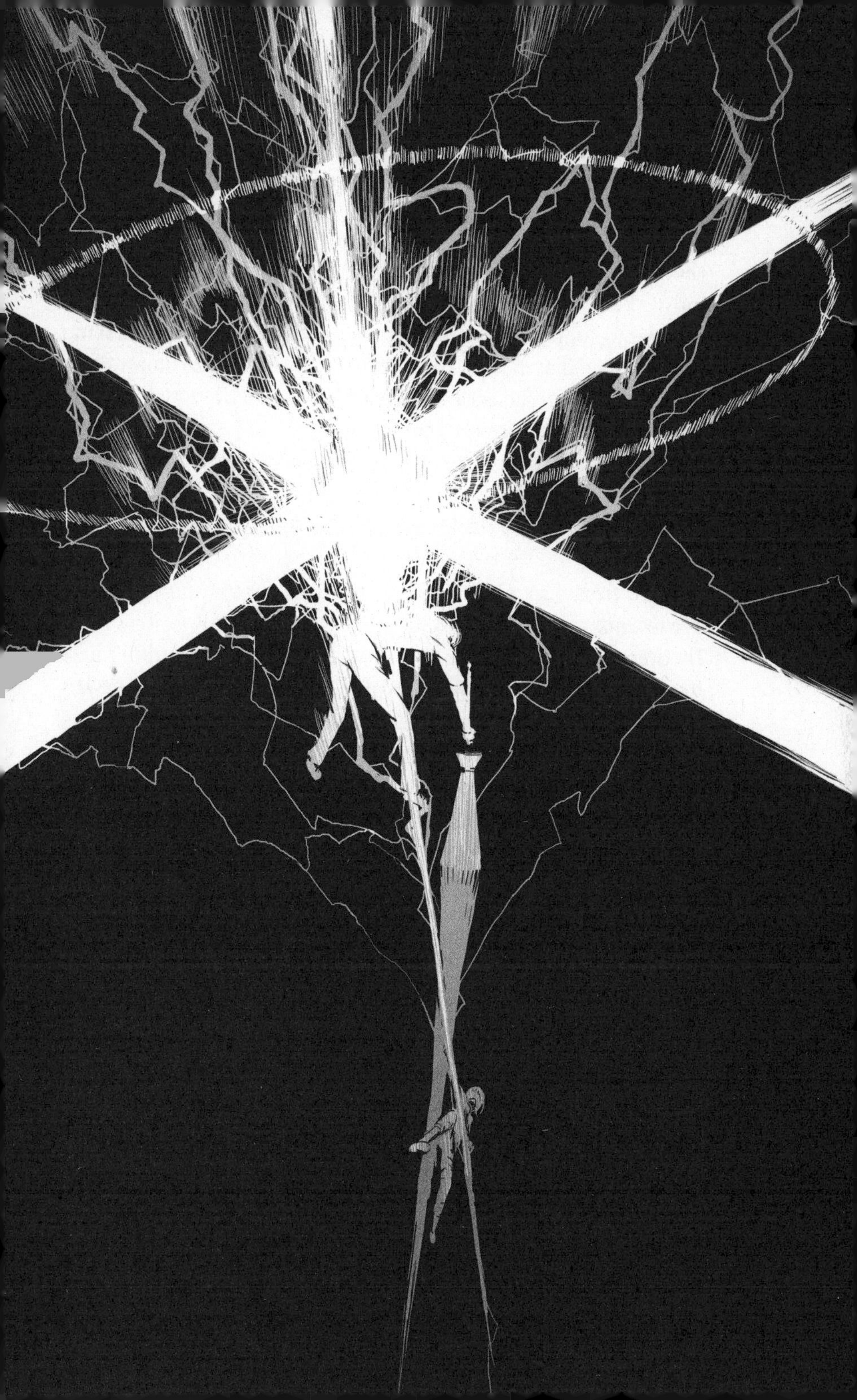

They would one day attain enough strength to no longer be a burden to her.

This time, they would gain the power to chase after her, grab her by the hands, and tell her it was all right.

The blood, sweat, and tears they'd shed culminated in the Saintbreaker.

In order to support her as a saint, they had to properly understand her as a saint. They had to overcome that wall, had to stand up to problems that even she, as a saint, was threatened by.

It was something that was genuine, real.

It was something only the Amakusa-Style Crossist Church had successfully devised.

A unique attack spell that existed for the sole purpose of defeating saints.

He'll be frozen in place because of his berserk mana for maybe thirty seconds.

Theoretically, this spell only worked on saints and wouldn't have any effect on normal sorcerers. Because of that, there were never any saints around who would purposely risk themselves as test subjects, meaning this was its first-ever usage.

But Itsuwa had definitely felt it hit. She calculated the effective time from that. *We'll use all our time to fully neutralize Acqua, now that he's a normal human!!*

However—

"That was a good spell."

This time, Itsuwa's face really froze.

Her Friulian spear, which had become a bolt of lightning, had, at some point, returned to its normal form. Itsuwa hadn't told it to. The spell had been calculated and disengaged by an outside power.

Acqua's left hand was at his stomach.

He wasn't pressing on a wound. His palm now held Itsuwa's spear, which was a mere hair from touching his skin. Right before her spear had changed into lightning, Acqua must have grabbed its tip with his hand. With the alteration before it went off, the special lightning bolt had veered off, ever so slightly.

"If I had been a normal saint, that might have gotten me."

Acqua's lips curled up. Not in scorn—but in a deep smile, displaying his joy at having met such strong opponents.

"It was very close."

Still controlling Itsuwa's spear with only his left hand, he moved his right. And the hunk of metal that was itself a mace, over five meters long.

"But I am both a saint *and* of God's Right Seat!!"

Da-pahh!! A roar reverberated throughout District 22.

She didn't even have the chance to use her clothing substitution spell. By the time she realized the noise had come from her own body, she'd already stopped breathing. Struck from above, her body launched into the thick, bulletproof fiber screen in less than a second, ripping it open and hurtling her the rest of the twenty meters to the ground.

"Gah— *Aaaaahhhhhhhhhhhhhhhhhhhh!!*"

As Itsuwa fell, she saw the glow of defensive spells spreading around her. It must have been her comrades. Itsuwa used what she had, too, desperate to build a spell that would decrease her speed. Unfortunately, her body crashed through all of it and slammed into the asphalt.

A gray dust cloud billowed up like smoke.

As her broken body lay half-buried in the shattered asphalt, she managed to move her neck and look up. Past the screen, torn this way and that, she heard something burst. *Za-bshhh!!* It sounded like a wave crashing against a boulder, but by the time she heard it, a huge geyser of water had already spurted from the screen's fissures. The several dozen tons of water looked like a giant arm, like a dragon's jaws. The members of Amakusa scattered into the air below, crushed by the sheer quantity. She heard several screams.

But she saw one person float to the ground like a feather.

"How dull. You came in full force, formulated a plan, and now you're done?"

It was Acqua. He put a foot on a piece of asphalt near Itsuwa, who was almost completely broken, speaking quietly.

"You still have several hours before the time limit I set."

The water fell like a waterfall from above the screen they used as a planetarium, causing mechanical warning alarms to go off everywhere. But Acqua was unperturbed. He looked down at Itsuwa with perfect composure, as though it were natural he would crush any enemy who came to him.

"I give you this choice. Hand over the boy's right arm, or stain the road with your blood."

"..."

He didn't get an answer.

But there was movement. She grabbed a cracked fragment of asphalt, forcing her bloodied and broken body to move, and tried to stand up.

"Then I have no choice," said Acqua quietly, bringing his huge mace around again. "If it is death you desire, then you will vanish in the waves."

His mace's tip pointed at her head.

Boom!!

In answer to Acqua's call, a vast amount of water that truly threatened to crush the fourth stratum cascaded from the screen above like a waterfall. It was a little under twenty meters long, shaped like a giant hammer with joints. Like the arms on construction vehicles it curved, as though it were aiming for both its prey, who had crawled up out of the ground, and the very lands themselves.

Itsuwa didn't close her eyes.

And that was why, at the very last moment, she noticed it.

Acqua's hand had suddenly stopped.

But she still felt an unknown murderous intent fill her surroundings.

It came not from Acqua of the Back; nor the other Amakusa members like Tatemiya and Ushibuka who had fallen nearby; nor Itsuwa, whose entire body was covered in wounds. It was a simple sensation of hostility, with an unknown range and direction. Acqua stopped himself and moved his attention away from his target. Something that even he, such a man as he was, would need to take caution of, was very close.

"...I see," murmured Acqua, before cracking a smile.

She'd seen that up close before—the look he gave to a strong opponent. But this time, the smile was many, many times deeper.

The tons of water roiling through the air of the fourth stratum broke. Without any magical control on it, the water sunk toward the artificial rivers, scattering huge, tidal wave–like ripples, putting the embankments underwater.

Acqua relaxed, then put his giant mace back on his shoulder.

Then, just once, he looked at Itsuwa. "You've kept your life. Thank your master for that."

Bam!! A burst. By the time she heard it, Acqua of the Back was gone. He went far too fast for her to follow with her naked eye.

She stared at the emptiness in front of her in complete bafflement.

She'd survived.

Given the disaster here with the ruined asphalt and concrete, the wreckage from all the water making it look like a bomb went off, she wasn't happy. Still, that was a vague conclusion; she didn't know if they'd won or lost. Without knowing how to judge the situation, Itsuwa simply repeated what Acqua had said.

"Thank...my master...?"

She craned her neck to look around. She wanted to follow where the man had looked to before, but nothing was there. It was gone, vanished just like Acqua, with only darkness there now.

9

A place about two hundred meters from the road where Itsuwa had fallen:

The hardened riverbanks of concrete had been turned into a small observation platform. Because of the Opila, the warding spell, there wasn't a soul to be seen in the cold facility—save for a pair of saints.

One was Acqua of the Back.

The other…

"I see you've been taking good care of my friends."

A tall body and fair skin. Black hair, tied at the back, reaching down to her waist. A T-shirt, tied up at the waist, with a denim jacket over top and jeans. The jacket's right sleeve, however, was cut off at the shoulder, and in contrast, the left pant leg of her jeans was cut off at the thigh.

Her outfit was plenty unique—but it all paled in comparison to a single item she carried.

A single sword, fastened to a western-style belt.

A Japanese katana, over two meters long, dubbed the Seven Heavens Sword.

"Yes, I believe I have heard of a saint in the Far East living by the creed of one-hit kills." Acqua nodded in satisfaction.

Saints who were affiliated with nations or organizations couldn't exactly go wherever or do whatever they liked. And yet, this one had accepted the risks to stand before him.

Acqua reaffirmed his grip on the mace.

At last, it wouldn't be bullying anymore. He could finally revel in a true fight.

"I believe I've also heard that the Amakusa saint is one who dislikes battle. Do you have what it takes to fight me?"

"Yes."

She—

"I still feel the same way. But it would seem I'm far more immature than I would have led myself to believe."

—Kaori Kanzaki.

"Perhaps it's because you made such a vivid show of routing them. Why, I'm almost ashamed of myself, despite my magic name. Despite having been taught that wrath is one of the seven deadly sins."

The saint, once called Priestess…

…simply ruled over this place as if she would blow away the very darkness that sat among its wreckage.

"My tedious worrying ends now. I will not let their determination be in vain. That's all I need."

For the sake of the boy who had been unfairly hurt.

For the sake of her friends, trampled by overwhelming force when they tried to stop him.

She gripped her katana's hilt almost tightly enough to crush it.

The two saints' gazes clashed.

That was the signal.

A battle between two monsters, whose ranks numbered under twenty in the whole world, was now under way.

INTERLUDE TWO

The Knights of Orleans.

France's largest sorcerer's society. That was the name that had taken all hope from the boy.

Originally, this group, attracted to Joan of Arc's personality, wasn't an official fighting force. It consisted of volunteers gathered to support her journey from the shadows. Nor were they a unique group specializing in magic. As long as a person abided the goal of saving France, their position, social standing, and family didn't matter. The group was *supposed* to have been—in an extremely rare instance at the time—a place for nobles and farmers alike to stand shoulder to shoulder and laugh among one another.

But on May 30, 1431, something happened that distorted the group's direction forever.

Joan of Arc was captured by England and burned at the stake as a heretic.

After that, the Knights of Orleans twisted into a strange group bent on vengeance. One of their goals was, of course, the destruction of all England, who had been the ones to personally execute her. But the targets of their revenge reached very far and wide, including French soldiers and nobles for not taking any real action to steal her back—despite having been saved by her—and even French civilians, who, strictly speaking, couldn't have done anything if they'd wanted to. But their group wasn't about to accept extenuating circumstances.

Though they were indeed the largest sorcerer's society in France, turning everyone against them at once meant their prospects of victory were grim. And they should have realized that fact, but they hadn't.

The Knights of Orleans had a single hope.

Joan of Arc hadn't been born with any special talents. When she was thirteen, she began hearing a strange voice, which is what led to an immediate blossoming of her ability.

After her death, the Knights still desired that ability, which they called the Revelations of Arc.

Not to defend anyone as she had done—but simply to sate their own vengeance.

Why had nobody realized that God would not help any who wished for miracles for their own personal gain? As a necessity, the Knights transformed into a group dealing in mysticism, and its distinctive features began to smell ever more of sorcery.

After hundreds of years and many generations of Knights, and their esoteric knowledge continuously passed down from one to the next, they were still continuing their experiment that would never work—the artificial mass production of those with Arc's power.

One boy and one girl were born in the midst of that.

The girl was chosen, if mostly by force, as a "subject" for the Revelations of Arc. The boy opposed it. He thought of plan after plan to let the girl escape, using all the strength he had to fight—and he'd failed.

She was no longer at his side.

The last thing the dying boy had heard was the girl's voice, saying, "I believe in you."

But the boy didn't have the strength to stand.

If he had, he would have used it a long time ago.

His body lay collapsed on filthy ground in a decaying alley.

"Do you plan on crawling there until death, giving up on everything?"

He heard a voice.

It was the tough-looking man claiming to be a freelance mercenary. He'd come to France to stop the Knights of Orleans' tyranny. There, he had met the boy and the girl, and had made a diversion of himself in order to let the girl escape...but the boy was far too weak and had let them take the girl away.

"What am I...supposed to do?" muttered the boy.

If he stretched out his hand, he could reach his sheathed sword. His colichemarde. A lightweight French short sword, modified from the sabers used in sporting events so that the boy could wield it in one hand. But that hand was a mess. He hesitated to even touch the sheath, as though it were boiling-hot water.

"I'm...not anyone special. I can't overcome every crisis just by using what happens to be around me!! There's no way I can win. I'm up against the strongest sorcerer's society in France! How the hell am I supposed to fight them?!"

"Will you give up on her, then?"

"..."

"Are you not still crawling on the ground here, moving toward her, because you can't accept that?"

"..."

The boy didn't answer. Couldn't answer.

Somehow, he worked his wound-covered, dirt-caked body and sat himself up, but that was all he could do. It wasn't just stamina he was missing—it was willpower.

The mercenary didn't act concerned for him. "This isn't the time to wallow in hopelessness."

No matter how long went by, he didn't pick the boy up. He took his sheathed sword in hand.

"The enemy is strong, and considering their ability to accomplish their goal, the girl's fate is clear. I should think there is only one thing you need to have on your mind right now."

"In other words," the mercenary said, "how she said she believed in you, despite this hopeless situation."

* * *

Time stopped within the boy. The only thing that continued was the mercenary's words:

"What will you do? Get up again to protect the dreams of a foolish girl? Or teach the foolish girl the truth and grant her even deeper despair?"

The mercenary gripped the sheath, his face almost up against the boy's, thrusting the sword's hilt against him—that colichemarde he was to wield courageously.

"Choose. What is your decision?"

It didn't need worry.

It didn't need thought.

There was a mountain of problems piled up before him. The risks were all over, scattered this way and that, numerous as the stars. But it didn't matter. Only those who had done something were allowed to think about those things.

The boy stood.

He ignored his wound-covered flesh, grabbed the hilt of the sword, undid the slender clasp holding it in place, and pulled his weapon from its sheath.

"A good choice."

The mercenary smiled.

The boy's expression had changed. He walked next to the man, standing as his exact equal, as comrades-in-arms. They walked to the dark alley's exit, their sights set on the enemy they needed to defeat and the hideout holding the girl they needed to save.

"Let's go," said the boy quietly.

"The time for fear is over."

Their enemy was France's largest sorcerer's society, the Knights of Orleans. A group of combat professionals driven by historical vengeance. But this would be the start of their real counterattack.

CHAPTER 3

Death Match of Monsters on a Different Level

Saint_vs._Saint.

1

Have you ever heard the sound of the world breaking?

The world's screams of pain. Beyond explosions and shock waves, destruction far beyond the range of human hearing? Only the fragments of aftermath compounded onto aftermath finally became explosive blasts humans could see. But those screaming fragments now blew away the street-side tree branches, rocked the fourth stratum's concrete ground, and bent the metal railings like they were sculptured candy.

Kaori Kanzaki and Acqua of the Back.

Their magical clash was all and everything on the observation platform that night, surrounded on all sides by science.

"Oooahhhhhh!!" With a shout, Kanzaki used a god-speed quick-draw technique. A strike certain to kill even angels, made by subverting spells used in one dogma against another.

A Buddhist spell for what a Crossist spell couldn't do.

A Shinto spell for what a Buddhist spell couldn't do.

A Crossist spell for what a Shinto spell couldn't do.

By covering for each one's weaknesses in the next timely cast, her attack techniques were second to none, delivering perfect, interlocking destruction.

It was, in other words, a single glint of light.

Her slashing attack was one nobody could have stopped—but Acqua repelled it with his giant mace. Several exchanges later, Kanzaki knew: Acqua had just as versatile a set of spells as she did, if not more so—and he did it by fully executing his ability to use regular magic, said to be impossible for God's Right Seat members.

When Kanzaki tried to detour to a Buddhist spell, he responded, and when she converted it to a Shinto spell, he immediately changed his defensive form. Vast amounts of mana shifted and switched between them, developing into a supersonic hand-to-hand battle in the midst of a parallel mental battle, with each reading the other's moves on a different dimension.

Physics and sorcery.

Flesh and mind.

Disturbance and meditation.

Gagagazazazazagigi!! Sparks flew in this battle of two saints as their weapons clashed. They appeared at first to be parallel but then showed a certain large undulation within.

In general, to use sorcery, one needed talent. The craft truly showed the skill difference when those without talent tried to create the same miracles as those with talent.

But could anyone say that after watching their movements? After seeing the incredibly exceptional, abnormal talent of the saints?

"...Wonderful. Such popularity. For this many men, this much strength, to come running to his aid alone. That boy may be my enemy, but I am impressed," noted Acqua, easily swinging around his five-meter-plus iron chunk like a tree branch. "However, you should prepare yourself. If you stand on my battlefield, your only path leads to destruction!!"

Grah!! A new explosion.

Behind Kanzaki flowed a dark river. By the time she noticed the black surface had shaken, a water pillar had already risen, close to twenty meters tall. It was a giant hammer with joints. The terrible weapon grazed the underground city's ceiling, closing down on Kanzaki's head.

If she had had her hands full merely with Acqua's other attacks, she wouldn't be able to deal with this one, and she'd die.

However…

Dbah!! A splitting sound rang out as their death match unfolded, and something near Kanzaki gave off a glare.

The moment he saw it, seven slashing attacks had brutally sliced up the water hammer approaching from behind, sending it back into the river.

It had been Seven Glints, using her wires.

"…I'm surprised you would think this was my full strength."

The instant her lips moved, the seven slashing attacks all converged on Acqua from various directions, as though complementing the track of her katana.

Acqua's chain of attacks sped up.

Some he repelled with his mace, and others he moved his head out of the way to dodge. Having overcome both her katana and wires, he saw—a sudden crimson flame obscure his vision.

"…?!"

The wires streaking through the air had created a three-dimensional magic circle. By the time Acqua realized this, the flames of the explosion had already engulfed his stalwart body.

A second blast followed, and then a third, with the seven wires slicing up through the blasts. They were finally followed by a single flash of a katana bathed in moonlight.

It didn't sound like a chain of attacks. It had been entirely too fast; the noises all rolled into a numberless clump.

Bang!! The roar was like a giant arm had torn through space itself.

But Acqua was no longer there. Kanzaki's gaze shifted to a distant spot in front of her. He was on the concrete ground, about ten meters away, having jumped back.

A single cut appeared on his cheek.

A slight graze, probably caused by a wire. But any wound was more than anyone had reached before now. As a drop of red blood trickled down his cheek, Acqua spoke quietly. "You *are* one of the Amakusa. What you're doing is fundamentally the same as them."

He fingered the flowing blood, then pressed that index finger onto the side of his mace, scrawling words onto it.

"And yet it changes so much when done by a saint. I am ever more stricken by the cruelty of talent."

Sorcery was a history of rebellion caused by those without talent. However, the word from the heavens, *saint*, easily quashed all of it.

The words gave Kanzaki slight pause.

"…"

Looking simply at the result, his complaint might have been correct. Without her, Amakusa couldn't even scratch Acqua.

However…

"Allow me to correct you," she said, sheathing her katana. She lowered her center, preparing for a quick-drawing strike. "They can't use Single Glint. But its foundations—the sword techniques, the wires, the spells, their combinations and tactical patterns—were all taught to us by the precursors of the Amakusa. The result has nothing to do with something as trivial as *talent*. It is a crystallization of history they've built. My school was the Amakusa. My masters were my friends. I will not allow you to speak ill of them."

Criiick!! The hand gripping the katana hilt filled with power.

"Moreover, a brute aware of all the power he holds mercilessly beating a mere high school student with it has no right to look down on others."

On reflection, those words dug into Kanzaki as well. It was an admonishment of herself as well, for once having attacked that same boy for a certain purpose.

"…The very fact that my words should anger you is proof of your indulgence," said Acqua, slowly bringing his mace back up, now with a pattern drawn on it in his own blood.

The ten meters between them was no more than a hairbreadth for the saints. Watching them face off against each other was like watching a classic western film.

A film of long-past halcyon days.

"The foot soldiers who have just begun their reconnaissance when they suddenly encounter an enemy tank—that is a battlefield.

Countermeasures are not always prepared in advance. There are no routes of escape, no safe zones, and certainly no gentlemanly manners. If you align all the same conditions, adjust the outcome to be fifty-fifty, what you are doing is not fighting—it is sport. That's how talent is. How power is. If soldiers encounter a tank without appropriate equipment, one does not need to ask what happened to the soldiers. They will be brutally bombarded and crushed. Is your battlefield different?"

"That way of thinking is your own."

"You and the others have nevertheless tread into such territory," said Acqua calmly, without so much as a sneer. "In the boy's case, actually, was there someone, somewhere, pulling him up?"

"..."

There was no signal, no advance notice before Kanzaki moved.

She charged up close to Acqua with such speed that even a professional sorcerer would have seen only a blur. Sparks flew like an explosion behind her, trailing after her as her sheath's tip scraped against the concrete ground. But before they could catch up, the unleashed Seven Heavens Sword mercilessly flew toward Acqua.

Ga-keeeeen!! A shrill metallic noise rang out. Kanzaki's and Acqua's weapons clashed, and they glared at each other from up close.

"You know all that! You know he's just a normal person caught up in this! Why, then, did you use your powers as a saint against him?!" she cried, her emotion on full display, something one wouldn't hear normally.

Perhaps it was because they were both saints. Or maybe it was because as saints, they shouldered a heavy past, one where they'd hurt many people.

"You know what happens when you wield that power, which not even twenty people in the world have—that power that strikes fear even into real sorcerers! Were you ignoring that when you went through with these atrocities?!"

"What would you do if I told you my reason for fighting?" In contrast, Acqua was completely calm and lucid. "For one who acts with conviction, excuses as to the path he's walked are unnecessary. My actions will speak with their results, for how much truth can there be in a play with only dialogue?"

Between them in their heated contest, the bloody letters on the side of the mace ignited a small explosion of manifested mana. The saints used the chance to put distance between themselves and regroup.

Kanzaki winced slightly, and Acqua readied his giant mace again, posture unchanging.

He was a strong opponent who would not falter; he likely had a single conviction supporting him. But Kaori Kanzaki couldn't even get a glimpse of it.

"Show me, saint of the Far East."

Acqua's body, his inner presence, instantly grew two sizes larger. It wasn't an issue of solely muscle, either. It was as though the mace he held, from tip to tip, had grown heavier and increased in pressure.

"Show me that those are more than just words. Show me the reason within your blade. Show me without words."

The saints clashed again.

With speed that none could follow and with power none could attain.

2

Touma Kamijou's eyelids moved.

It was so slight that it didn't seem like he'd done it on purpose. It was more along the lines of a spasm, as he slowly, very slowly, cracked his eyelids open. But even then, he didn't acquire vision for a few seconds. His focus and perspective wavered, until finally, his brain perceived what looked like a hospital ceiling.

...Whe...where...?

He didn't know where he was. Even if he'd seen the place before, his brain might not have been processing his visual information. His nose picked up the scent of disinfectant alcohol more quickly than his mind figured out what he was seeing.

...What...happened...?

He felt adhesive tape on his chest and abdomen. Electrodes were probably attached to them for taking readings.

The lights in the room were dimmed, but he felt someone else here. A subtle pressure near the middle of his bedding...

His eyes moved in that direction, where he found Index sleeping on a pipe chair next to the bed. He couldn't see her face through her long hair, but she'd probably been here for a while now.

It gave him a very slight prick of pain.

"..."

A little bit of energy returned to his limply hanging hand.

He could tell the blood was circulating to his head in response to regaining consciousness.

Acqua of the Back.

Itsuwa.

The Amakusa.

Kamijou had passed out after being launched from the suspension bridge, but their battle must have still been going on. He hoped it was. Of course, there was a chance, albeit very slim, that the Amakusa had already won, and it was over. Unfortunately, he couldn't see that happening—Acqua was genuinely a monster. He knew there was nothing a high school student like him could do if he stood up to the man, but it would obviously be better for them to have as much combat strength as they could.

Acqua had viewed the power in his right hand as dangerous.

That meant he still had the chance to influence the battle if he used it.

His right hand, which could even erase miracles from God.

He gave it a look, then nodded.

He looked at Index again, slumped on top of his bed and sleeping.

The girl, keenly and earnestly worried about him.

...I'm sorry, Index. I'll apologize later; I'll apologize to death...

And yet:

So please, just let me do what I need to right now.

3

Pow!! An explosion ripped through the Academy City night.

It wasn't from flames. It was a shock wave from a massive eruption of water.

Acqua had used sorcery to control the vast stores of river water, creating a giant hammer that almost scraped against the underground city's ceiling. Kanzaki's wires cut through it brutally. Tons of water in the shape of a construction arm were instantly vaporized, sending steam everywhere. But Acqua controlled that steam in turn, converting it into a glittering cloud of diamond dust.

He had more than just a hammer at his beck and call. The entire fourth stratum, almost two kilometers across, was already in his grasp. Artificially laid rivers made completely dry, every drop of them floating in the air. It formed a slender line, drawing itself across the entire stratum and forming a complex, wondrous magic circle.

With each formation, switch, and re-creation of the magic circle, another barrage of varied spells came to Acqua's aid.

Attacks of all shapes and sizes assaulted Kanzaki.

Several spears of ice, each close to thirty meters long, flew at her.

A watery tail, undulating like a whip, lashed out at her from various angles.

A giant, ball-shaped mass swung down at her, then swept out to the side.

And Acqua himself, slipping through the cracks, made his way up to Kanzaki.

His strategy: combine several attacks, each of which was a one-hit kill move, and then send her chances of death skyrocketing even further. By Acqua's prediction, after seventy seconds, Kanzaki should have lost enough speed for him to land a fatal wound.

"!!"

But even after that time had elapsed, Kanzaki counterattacked.

In response to the watery magic circle changing its form over and over, Kanzaki spread her seven wires out in all directions, immediately creating a bounded field to deal with it. She was prepared to be his lesser in true ability, so she sometimes cut through the water jets, sometimes dove inside one to bend its path and cause his spell to fail, and sometimes hijacked one mid-cast, using it for herself.

It was like electronic warfare—magical hacking.

Water and wires. The two networks tore each other apart, created openings, outwitted each other, all in an effort to sap their limited world's ability.

Countless rays of light painted the world. The water Acqua's magic circles constructed, and the wires Kanzaki used to break it. Acqua, who filled the entire underground city, and Kanzaki who stood alone in a space inside it.

As they carried out this staggering battle of sorcery in their minds, they also pushed forward with direct hand-to-hand martial combat in parallel. They performed feats in one battle or the other that normal sorcerers wouldn't be able to follow if they were fully focused, and they did both at the same time.

Explosions burst through the air. The space between Kanzaki and Acqua began to haze. Steel across steel, swung from different directions, intersecting and colliding.

He uses the Adoration of Mary... While wielding her katana and her wires simultaneously, Kanzaki clenched her teeth. It wasn't merely pain causing the expression.

A special law that twisted the rigid rules of Crossist techniques: That was how Acqua had explained it, but the Adoration of Mary was for something else to begin with. It was a chance for the defeated to rise again. Whether a person had broken the rules and strayed from the path by committing a sin or causing tragedies terrible enough to abandon God, the image of the Virgin Mother would shed tears for their sake, smile to them in their dreams, and grant them the ability to carry out miracles. People everywhere used that as a starting point, devoting their minds to prayer, and in doing so, unconsciously used the spell.

It was said that was how certain people could spread chaotic miracles about. They would be misunderstood as worshipping someone other than the Son of God, but that was wrong. The true nature of the Adoration of Mary was that it stopped the tragedies that happened in the gaps of the network built by the Church and the clergy. Mary didn't put Crossist society out of order. There was simply enough of a reason for people to kneel and pray for the safety of their family, their friends, their comrades.

Mary.

The highest saint in history—the one who had performed the greatest feat in all of Crossist history—giving birth to Christ. She'd accepted the angel's words so she could grant the people relief and salvation, conceived Jesus, and prepared herself for a path laden with trials alongside her husband. And the Adoration was the crystallization of that faith, created by the feelings of those who adored her.

And that.

Those feelings…!!

Logical interpretation of the Adoration of Mary spell, which was displayed in the form of straightforward, simple prayer, was difficult, and there were many reports of stone statues that depicted her being miraculous items, while completely missing the mark. The streets were rampant with swindlers, too, using that fact to their own ends. But Acqua was even crueler than they. He was creating actual miracles and using them to commit atrocities.

"You are quite something," came Acqua's voice amid the thunderous claps of clashing longsword and blunt weapon. "To think you would bring two kilometers and five thousand tons of magic circle to submission using feats of strength.

"But," he continued, "it looks to me as though your body has already passed its limit."

"?!"

When his indication caused Kanzaki's movements to dull slightly, Acqua's attacks increased in intensity and rained down on her. The difference between them seemed ready to open wide in the blink of an eye, but she swung her sword again, meaning to turn the tables.

When activating Single Glint, Kanzaki forcibly drew out power exceeding the momentum her physical body could control. There was no way for her to fight for long in such a state, meaning her

Single Glint had been polished by necessity into a sword-drawing technique that would end the contest in a single moment.

But such instant-kill techniques didn't work on Acqua.

He stood before her as a saint, with power equal to or greater than her own, and on top of it, he also held the mark of God's Right Seat, radically powering up his body. Kanzaki could only step into this world for a few moments; Acqua of the Back advanced through it steadily.

She bit down. It was almost like he was an angel.

Acqua of the Back presided over the power of Gabriel.

Even Misha Kreutzev only seemed to achieve imperfect manifestation...By odd coincidence, she'd fought the real archangel of that name once before. *But this is still strange. I sense something more than that from Acqua...Urgh?!*

This string of attacks seemed too much for a saint with similar capacity. Acqua felt as though he rivaled that archangel, imperfect though it may have been.

But how was that possible?

Could he really store so much power without destroying himself?

"Hnn!!"

She heard him exhale. For a moment, an odd, floating sensation enveloped her. Eventually, she realized that he'd stopped his relentless chain, then stored up energy to attack again. But by that time, his full-power strike was upon her.

The giant mace came down hard at her from directly overhead; Kanzaki positioned her katana horizontally to stop it. When they clashed, a *shhh-thud* went off, sending an enormous shock rattling through her katana to her arms, her torso, and down to her feet all at once, causing her boot soles to dig inches into the ground. It was hard tile underfoot, but she sunk into it like it was mud. The attack hadn't struck her head, but she felt herself waver, as though it had shaken her brain.

But she endured it.

And the moment after Acqua's mighty attack, with all his weight behind it, there would come an opening.

"Ooooohhhhhh!!"

With a roar, Kanzaki followed through with her Seven Heavens Sword.

Perfect timing; a pristine opportunity: a move to pull herself back from the brink of disaster.

Acqua's mace stopped even that. *Ga-keeeen!!* A dull shock wave proclaimed far and wide that it had dispersed the power behind her katana.

"It has been three years since the last battle of saints. Such a long time. This has been good exercise." At close range, Acqua gave an emotionless smile. "But let's end this. I came here to do a job. I have no time to amuse myself with *sport*."

"?!"

Unable to properly respond, Kanzaki pulled back her katana and swung even harder, delivering a relentless attack.

But Acqua wasn't in front of her.

She sensed him with her mind, rather than her vision: Her target was above.

He had jumped about twenty meters up. A leap like a rocket launch, impossible for normal people. Becoming a single point in the air, he placed the satellite representing the power of Gabriel, the moon, at his back.

Strictly speaking, he didn't. It was only the planetarium screen, torn to shreds, displaying the night sky.

When he got near the ceiling, Acqua turned himself one hundred and eighty degrees, then placed his feet on the artificial canopy.

"!!" Kanzaki immediately tried to pursue, but the damage from earlier—and, most of all, the strain on her body that she'd been accumulating—created a few instants' lag.

Stopped in place, a chill surrounded her from all sides. It was the rhythm of life and death, which only true warriors could sense. One could glimpse it when the entire flow of the battle had shifted, shaken. Like the slanting of a seesaw that didn't physically exist.

And overhead was Acqua.

"The Holy Mother mitigates severe punishment."

In response to his whispers, the moon hanging behind him gave off a burst of light. No—the mechanism displaying video on the planetarium screen had come under some kind of load and shorted out. *Crack-snap!!* Several sparks escaped, as though ticking down a countdown to the unknown.

No normal sorcerer could use that sort of logic—but Acqua's Adoration of Mary forced it to work.

This is...!! The bluish-white flash enveloped the steel mace, and she could tell it was storing an immense amount of power.

"This power, which at times appeals directly to God's law. Let it wrap you in mercy and ascend to heaven!!"

With a cry, he kicked the ceiling away from him and lunged downward. The already damaged false sky collapsed in its entirety from the strike, and the blue tranquility returned to a jet-black darkness.

A straight-line descent.

And a giant mace swinging down at her.

What unleashed from there was not a slash, nor a stab, nor a firing, nor an explosion, nor a burst, nor a severing, nor a crushing.

It was simple pressure.

The overwhelming destructive force pushing down surpassed even a small planetary collision.

All sound vanished from the world then.

Even the sound of the world breaking was gone.

In a circle one hundred meters around Acqua, the ground of Academy City District 22's fourth stratum found itself brutally razed by his massacring attack. The descent's impact didn't even let a crater form—it simply smashed the steel and concrete ground to bits, transforming it into a giant hole.

It didn't matter if the ground had shelter-level toughness or anything else.

The destroyed land across that hundred-meter circle merely rained down into the fifth stratum below.

Explosions, quakes, and so much dust.

The sequence of smashing and crashing echoed on and on.

Water poured down like a waterfall; the rivers and water power generator pipes had been severed.

"Guh...urgh..."

Amid it all lay Kaori Kanzaki.

She'd stopped the attack itself with her Seven Heavens Sword, but the ground beneath her feet hadn't been able to withstand it.

The immense pressure had cast her down, along with a mountain of rubble, from a height of over twenty meters. Now, she lay faceup on a chunk of concrete.

Her body was in tatters. Even though Acqua's attack hadn't landed a direct hit, its pressure went through her weapon to damage her. She'd been caught between his extra-large mace and the man-made ground, and now a dark red liquid dripped from every part of her—from her arms, from her legs, from her torso.

One of the saints had been brought to *this*.

Immediately, she realized that if she was hit with that again, she would die.

However...

"..." As she grated her teeth in frustration, there was no fear or shock on her face.

Only anger.

She was directly below the crater, in the fifth stratum. She'd fallen into a large plaza, so thankfully, it didn't seem like the collapse had killed anyone. That, however, was merely being wise after the event. What if this had been a residential area? What if someone had happened to be walking through the plaza? Just thinking about it gave Kanzaki a chill down her spine. Academy City must have implemented some sort of measure, but unlike the fourth stratum, the bare minimum magical Opila ward wasn't even here.

He was a saint like her.

He had a talent not even twenty people in the world had.

Why was this absurdity the only place he wielded that power?

"Acqua...," she growled, dragging her upper body into a sitting position and snatching up her sword from where it had fallen atop the rubble.

Acqua of the Back had made a rough landing on the fifth stratum ground with her. "Where is the Imagine Breaker?" he asked, the mace that had caused this incredible destruction laid lightly on his shoulder. "Or will I meet him eventually if I crash through more strata?"

"Acquaaaaaaaaaaaaaaaaaaaaaaaaaaaaaaaaaaaaa!!"

Kanzaki blasted to her feet so forcefully, her own blood lashed out around her.

Her Seven Heavens Sword, held in a two-handed grip, wavered unsteadily. She'd clenched her fists so tightly that she'd broken several nails, and red blood dripped between her fingers. The immense impact she couldn't completely withstand had damaged her from the inside, and when she tried to take a breath, she ended up coughing up a chunk of blood.

But the light in her eyes was no weaker than before.

And as long as that light didn't fade, her blade would never stop.

Kanzaki let loose a roar to inspire herself, even to the point of squeezing her damaged organs. Acqua batted away her simultaneous attack—metal clanging against metal—then a chain of those metallic sounds, layered over one another, instantly caused the air to burst.

Ga-bam!! Sounds of clashing and collisions rang out.

The two saints crossed blades once more.

They were both so fast that the arrival of that observation would be late for the next strike.

Kaori Kanzaki swiftly swung her blade, dragging the seven wires through the gaps as though sewing, re-sheathing her katana at the slightest opportunity, then striking out with incredibly fast sword draws. At the same time, she created attack spells of flame and ice, continuously ambushing Acqua in an unpredictable pattern by combining three-dimensional magic circles made out of her wires, her footwork, and the rhythm of steel banging on steel.

In response, as soon as Acqua batted down her katana with his giant mace, he would suck in the night air and the fragments of moonlight within it—perhaps an attribute of Gabriel—and thereby increase his mace's power. He also used the properties of the Adoration of Mary, which mitigated severe punishment, to overcome the condition that God's Right Seat couldn't use ordinary sorcery. As he loosed a string of attacks that exceeded the speed of sound, he simultaneously used vacuum blades and chunks of rock to strike at Kanzaki from multiple angles.

Bagagagagazazazazazagigigigigi!! Sparks flew. A miniature starry sky danced around them.

"Guh, *uff*?!"

But the result was clear as day.

Blood spurted from Kanzaki's mouth at uneven intervals. She was already past her limit. She'd unmistakably taken severe damage in places on and in her body. The speed at which she wielded her blade diminished conspicuously, and now that she couldn't keep up, an image of a hopeless future flashed through her mind. She was devoting everything just to stay with him; there were no strikes she could make that would turn the tables—for turning the tables was something you could only do by keeping a card up your sleeve.

She had used all her cards, and they couldn't deal with him. She wouldn't have that chance. If she couldn't afford to keep even one trick up her sleeve, it wouldn't be possible to even the score.

But…

"I'm telling you…to shut…the hell up!!"

What came to mind next were the words he'd said when she'd first met him in Academy City.

Remembering them returned her strength.

It was all coming back:

"That's got nothing to do with it! Are you protecting people just because you feel like your strength obligates you?!"

The boy, who had stood up to a saint with a single clenched fist—all for their treatment of one girl named Index.

"That's not it, is it?! Don't fool yourself! You got that power because there was something you *wanted to protect!"*

She didn't exactly think his words were the most beautiful in the world. There were as many ideas as there were people, and none of them stood at the top of all the rest. That said, Acqua of the Back must have had his own reasons and beliefs that required him to fight.

However.

His reason—to mercilessly beat an ordinary person, even aware of his immense strength as a saint and of God's Right Seat—wouldn't let him beat that boy. She knew it.

The boy's actions, being *just* a boy but taking a hit from Acqua to protect Itsuwa, would never lose out to someone who dominated as though doing so was as natural as one of the "chosen ones."

As she wielded her blade, Kaori Kanzaki gritted her teeth.

The reason the boy had shown her.

The conviction he'd risked his life to show her.

She couldn't let this coward, with talent as his only possession, trample that.

4

The Amakusa-Style Crossist Church members, numbering almost fifty, paid no attention to their miserable state—the bandages they'd used to fix themselves up had been torn apart, redness seeping up through them—instead, they stood at the edge of the giant hole Acqua had punched in the fourth stratum, watching, dumbstruck, the battle unfolding between the two saints in the fifth.

The aftermath of the explosions, the blasts, and the shock waves were incredible on their own, and given the amount of debris scattered around them, it was a wonder no civilians had gotten caught up in it.

Despite being human, the overwhelming momentum and shock waves drove away even the raging vortex of mana as the monsters' duel unfolded. Roars sounded, clangs of metal on metal rang out, and the blasting winds blew out the vapor in the air, creating afterimages like condensation trails. Several flashes sparked between every single attack—a spell that would have turned any of those currently in Amakusa to ash with just one hit—and then that spell would be intercepted by another, in an endless cycle.

From their distant perspective, it looked like the collision of two galaxies. With the clash of the saints, stars exploded, space warped, planets were swallowed in darkness, and new lights were born, strong enough even to drive away that oppressive void. What, then, did the two standing at the center of those transient galaxies represent?

One of them was Kaori Kanzaki.

A woman who had once led the Amakusa, and who still gazed warmly upon them from the shadows.

The Amakusa's former Priestess was now fighting for them:

To save the civilian boy Acqua had designated as his target, as well as to save the current Amakusa members he had attacked.

But—

"…"

They heard a crash.

It was the sound of Itsuwa's Friulian spear slipping from her bloody hand as she gazed at the battle. The spear she'd poured every last drop of their skills into reinforcing in order to save one boy. It was the crystallization of her efforts—and now it lay on the ground, like a rock by the roadside.

It wasn't just Itsuwa.

Several others had dropped their weapons in the same way. Some of their knees gave out, and some of them put a hand on a wall. And they all had the same expression she did.

Absolutely spiritless.

What have I been doing this whole time? thought Itsuwa.

The more Kaori Kanzaki fought for their sake, the more it felt like a rejection of their hard work. No matter how hard they tried, they'd never step off the palm of their saint. She would look at them as if gazing at something dear to her, and if danger approached, she would fight to such heights that nobody could ever reach.

They'd never gotten him to *look* at them.

No matter how far it went, it was nothing but play to him.

They felt as though the harsh truth would crush them. At the same time, they felt so petty for not being able to think anything else of the life-risking kindness she'd shown them. And that loss would inevitably shatter them even further. But they couldn't do anything about it. They were like ants to a giant. They couldn't step into this incredible battle, and just watching it completely drained what little stamina and willpower still remained in their worn-out bodies.

If that boy was here, he wouldn't have cared.

If he'd seen a friend, Kaori Kanzaki, fighting before his eyes and being hurt—that would have been all it took for him to clench his fist and break right into the middle of the fight.

That was another kind of strength.

But right now, the Amakusa didn't have the conviction needed to display such a thing.

The battle between two saints continued.

Without realizing that even if their completely overwhelming strength wasn't hitting them directly, it was still gouging holes into the hearts of their audience.

INTERLUDE THREE

The distress signal had come long ago, but none of them could make a move.

It wasn't as though they were heavily wounded. It wasn't as though their destination was very far away, either. They couldn't move simply because of position and politics.

The distress signal had arrived from a British royal long-distance escort coach.

The horse-drawn coach's magical defensive net should have been perfect. It was so tough that ever since they'd made it, they joked that not even the planet tearing in half would cause it to emit a distress signal. It was far beyond the Walking Church, the special habit. England, the great land of magic, had used all its technology and history to design it, giving it the moniker Mobile Fortress. This coach, meant for the royal family, should never have been stopped, no matter who attacked it.

And it had sent them a distress signal.

Under normal circumstances, this was absolutely impossible.

It meant something very simple.

There had been a political deal of some sort.

And England's third princess on board was a piece that had been sacrificed.

The members of the Knights faction, on the national border along the Dover Strait, listened silently to the distress signal as it repeated, again and again, their hearts gripped with pain.

Nobody said a word, and everyone grated their teeth in frustration, clench their fists hard enough for blood to seep from their palms.

The Knights' goal was the prevention of internal schism within the United Kingdom—which possessed a complex relationship between three factions and four cultures—and to defend with their lives all who inherited enough royal blood to lead the kingdom.

The men of the Knights worked within that Machiavellian vortex, and because their environment was so harsh, so cruel, they could speculate as to their situation without needing any real explanation.

The Third Princess of England was under attack by the Spanish Order of the Star. They were an extremely large group within the Roman Orthodox Church, and ever since the Spanish Armada had been destroyed during the age of Elizabeth I, the magical factions of England and Spain had been at odds with one another.

The royal family had purposely allowed this attack to occur, likely because they desired a war with the Order of the Star. They'd been the ones to spread Crossism during the great age of exploration, and even now, the Order exercised almost complete influence over all the Catholic cultural factions in South America. England was trying to wrest influence in South America away from the Roman Orthodox Church's Spanish Order of the Star and thus extend their own sphere of influence. Further, the third princess didn't have much authority in the royal family. They'd probably weighed her against an entire continent and decided to sacrifice her.

It was the Knights' job to protect the princess. As a matter of course, they would run to her aid even when she didn't request rescue. Ignoring a distress signal from her was, normally, completely out of the question.

However.

Right now, at this exact moment, the Knights could be no more than rocks.

They'd been ordered to move with swiftness if the magical battle in France extended to England across the Dover Strait, but they were ordered—without reason—not to move unless those embers reached the homeland.

"..."

William Orwell left a tent the Knights had set up.

Even now, an intermittent light shone beyond the Dover Strait that night. It wasn't a lighthouse. It was the aftermath of the Spanish Order's magical attacks, escaping to them from over the French border.

"Are you going?"

A voice addressed him from behind.

William turned and saw the top of the Knights, the Knight Leader, standing there. Unlike the sturdily built Acqua, the man had an elegance about his behavior. It was likely thanks to his upbringing, in particular the fact that he'd needed to learn etiquette at castles and palaces. Which was only natural, given his expected, permanent role of defending those with royal blood.

William Orwell was a mercenary who would fight for anyone who hired him.

The Knight Leader would spend his life in service of his nation. They wouldn't normally be able to get along.

But in actuality, they would have drinks together whenever they had the chance. The Knight Leader had invited William into the Knights numerous times, and William had refused every time. But after fighting elsewhere in the world, he would naturally drift back to England to wet his throat with a cup. Everything about them was different, from their positions to their perspectives, from their fighting styles to their ways of life. And yet, strangely, they accepted each other.

Which was how the Knight Leader knew.

Knew what William was thinking when he left the tent without a word.

"You are fettered as ones who protect the nation. The actions of those with the nation at their back will represent the nation's will. You can't cross the border to France without orders and engage the Spanish."

William Orwell spoke quietly, adjusting the giant mace on his shoulder.

"But I am different. I am just a mercenary. I can run rampant all I like—I don't have the nation backing me. What I do will not reflect at all on England's intentions."

"You think I'll let you go on your own?" The Knight Leader's lips turned up. "You may be a storied veteran, but I can't leave this in your hands alone. Come—with your luck, you'll survive. But it's our duty to protect the princess; we can't entrust her to a mercenary of unknown origin. She might just be one kid, but she's an unmarried woman. If a lawless brigand kidnaps her, it puts the entire nation in danger."

"Did you not hear what I said?" William said, mildly shocked that the man's argument was nothing more than a farce. Still, he knew the Knight Leader was speaking out of consideration despite his joking tone.

When their eyes met, each knew what the other was thinking.

It was a bond they couldn't escape from.

"Yes, you said the Knights have all of Britain on their shoulders, so they can't intervene," said their leader simply, removing a pure gold decoration from his chest. His identification emblem—decorated with his family emblem, escutcheon in the center. The man gazed at it wistfully for just a moment, but eventually let it go.

Without returning his eyes to his emblem, now on the ground, he looked directly into William's eyes. "Now I've been disqualified from knighthood. Which means you're taking me with you. If the distress signal is still being sent, the third princess must still be alive."

"I see. How very like you."

William Orwell, now aware of his friend's determination, smiled slightly.

He'd probably known the Knight Leader would do that, too. He knew what kind of person this man was, this man with whom he'd shared drinks time and time again.

That was exactly why he entrusted his back to the man during fights.

The Knight Leader glared bitterly at the popping lights across the strait and urged William onward. "Let's hurry. It may not be able to move anymore, but its defenses should still be functional...The royal faction set it up personally, though, so we don't know how long it will stay that way. In any case, we need to rush there posthaste."

"You are right."

William candidly agreed, but a moment later, he'd rammed his fist deep into the Knight Leader's gut. With a dull *whump*, he looked at William with an expression of disbelief.

"What...are you...doing...?"

"No. I cannot take you with me. You know that."

William removed his fist, and the Knight Leader crumpled, as though he'd lost something holding him up. Still, it wasn't enough to knock the man out, trained as he was. William didn't watch as he struggled—he just spoke.

"I use my trivial position as mercenary to travel the world's battlefields at will. But even I cannot enter England's castles and palaces. That is something only you can do."

"Will...iam..."

"If you truly want to protect the third princess, you must look to the future, not just the present. The disaster that invited this strategic move will strike the third princess many more times in the future. When that happens, she had better have someone with her. Protect her, leader of knights. Not only the third princess, either, but the royal family as a whole, though rotten with such political horse-trading. That is the job you were given, as a knight—not I, a mercenary."

"William Orweeeelllllllllllllllllllllll!!"

Shrugging off the Knight Leader's shout from where he lay upon the ground, William headed to the battlefield.

The Knight Leader heard a magic name.

A certain mercenary's magic name.

"The time has come to name myself. My name is Flere210—the one who changes the reason for your tears!!"

The Dover Strait lay between England and France.

But William Orwell, equipped with spells that allowed him to move through the water, shot across the national border with the speed of a cannonball.

CHAPTER 4

The Protector and the Protected

Leader_Is_All_Members.

1

Mikoto Misaka trudged through the late-night streets.

She had been out using a bath facility to get the post-bath Croaker cell phone strap, but her timing had been poor. She'd happened across a dangerous event unique to District 22 called an "anoxic warning," stranding her inside a building. The next thing she knew, it was very late at night, she had impeccable post-bath chills, and she'd lost the reason to take a bath at all.

Gah, damn it...After all that, I guess I'll have to use the one in my dorm..., she'd thought—but for some reason, the exit to District 22 had been cordoned off.

It seemed as though the anoxic warning had settled for the moment, so the building-exit restriction had been lifted. Apparently, some system or other had malfunctioned. The middle-aged man managing the gate was just as confused as she was.

Normally, she'd want to put in a complaint, but she heard a lot of hurried footsteps behind the man, as well as deep shouts and reprimands flying back and forth. The face of the man who came to deal with her was also somewhat glum. She pitied him too much to pile on any more complaints, so she gave up the idea of snapping at him.

Weird. I wonder what happened.

Despite how she looked, Mikoto had just as much of a penchant for getting into other people's trouble as that boy. She worried a little about what was going on with that, too.

"Nyo-wah?!"

Suddenly, there came a crackling of static electricity from her bangs.

Her ability didn't have minor random misfires very often, so she quickly sent a polite smile to the surprised man in front of her, bowed, and left the place for the moment.

Maybe it was specific to Academy City, not being able to control your own ability, but it was surprisingly embarrassing in its own right. Still, this led her to stop wanting to stick her nose into wherever the trouble was.

If she had been familiar with sorcery, she might have realized the misfire was due to an Opila ward, which affected a person's senses and awareness, clashing with her own ability-controlling methods.

What on earth could that have been? she wondered. For now, she wouldn't be able to get back to the surface until the gate's malfunctions were fixed, so she looked at a sign with a map of District 22, then decided to make a visit to a rather high-class hotel on the seventh stratum.

I hope I can check into a room without any advance notice...And our R.A. is going to be low-key scary. Maybe I should call Kuroko and have her come here and get me out with her teleportation.

Meanwhile, she descended the spiraling, downward slope to the seventh stratum.

And then it happened.

A figure suddenly appeared before her in the darkness, moving as if floating. At the very least, they clearly weren't walking normally; their motions were less unreliable than unstable. She frowned. A maniac? But when the figure stepped under a streetlight, surprise washed over her face.

It was Touma Kamijou.

"What...What the heck are you doing?!" she called, rushing over to him.

Normally, she wouldn't have reacted like this. She knew the boy wandered around the streets at night on a daily basis, and they always seemed to run into each other one way or another. Maybe they'd fought sometimes, but she was seldom ever worried.

But right now, Mikoto faced a situation that forced her to divert from her usual behavioral patterns.

Touma Kamijou was clearly not well.

His face was pale, as though he'd been soaking in a sea of ice. The bandages wrapped all over him were coming off in certain places, probably due to the movement, and there was even redness seeping through in a few spots. His clothing was odd, too. It wasn't the familiar school uniform—all he wore was what looked like an operating gown for a surgical patient.

"Misaka…Is that you…?" groaned Kamijou, leaning against the lamppost, barely managing to hold himself up. There were electrodes taped to his cheeks and arm, with their cord ends hanging down to the ground, as though he'd ripped himself free.

Mikoto was shocked.

She had to look closely, but his left and right pupils were dilating slightly differently. They weren't completely focused. He was probably seeing everything in a blur, like through frosted glass.

From his expression, though, he didn't seem to realize it. Or maybe he was in such a fix that he couldn't afford to pay attention to such a trifle.

"…"

Kamijou's lips moved, but Mikoto couldn't make out what he'd said. He merely released the lamppost from his hand, motions slow, and began to move again. As he went to pass by her, his knees gave out.

She almost heard the pop as he nearly collapsed to the ground. Mikoto hastily moved to support him.

"You idiot!! Where did all those wounds come from? And are those electrode cords attached to you…? Don't tell me you broke out of some hospital or other, did you?!"

"I…have to go…" With them so close now, she finally heard his voice. "They're probably…still fighting. I…have to join them…"

Just those few sparse words made Mikoto's entire body shiver.

She'd guessed, one way or another, that this boy had been involved in several incidents Mikoto was unaware of. But she'd thought they were just simple extensions of street fights. Once before, she'd witnessed him fighting Academy City's strongest Level Five, but she considered that a once-in-a-lifetime thing. Who would have imagined him going through so many incidents that placed him on the verge of death?

At the same time, it made sense to part of her.

A single word crossed her mind.

...Amnesia.

If he kept on fighting like this, whittling away his own life every time, his body wouldn't be in perfect shape. Mikoto didn't know whether his amnesia was caused by mental trauma or a problem with his brain's construction. But unfortunately, she considered both of those possible. That was how badly his body was beaten up right now.

She had to stop him.

Stop him from dragging himself out here, looking like he was about to die; stop him from standing up to all these crisis situations, even after he'd lost his memories.

"...?" Kamijou stared at Mikoto in confusion. She wasn't letting go of his arm. He seemed to have no idea why she was just standing there. He'd been keeping everything that would make others worry a secret, so he thought it was impossible anyone would reach out to him. He honestly believed that it was just too convenient for someone to realize the trouble he was in and come to help him, even if he kept quiet.

That little thing made her angry.

Truly angry.

"Why...didn't you say anything?" Before she knew it, she was murmuring. She understood that she'd never be able to go back now, but she couldn't stop herself. "Say you need help! Say you need someone else! No, it doesn't even have to be that specific. Be even simpler!! Just say, for once in your life, that you're scared or uneasy about something!!"

"Misaka...what...are you...?"

"I know all about it."

Kamijou continued, even now, putting on an act in order to deceive her—no, to keep her from getting involved. She ignored it.

"I know you have amnesia!!"

That moment, Kamijou's shoulders twitched.

She thought she saw a wavering in him, a big one—one that greatly affected his life.

Mikoto herself felt a shock as she looked at him, standing there at a loss.

But so what?

Once before, this boy had literally saved her life. Not only her, either—all ten-thousand-odd of those girls she'd wanted to protect, too.

She'd been about to face Academy City's strongest Level Five when Touma Kamijou had appeared. And he'd done it in a way that'd stomped all over her innermost thoughts—of trying to carry everything herself until she died.

His method certainly didn't have a shard of delicacy, and it was even a greedy, swinish approach, considering how it invaded her privacy like that. But for Mikoto Misaka and her Sisters, it had still saved them.

She wouldn't allow Touma Kamijou to deny that way of doing things.

It should be fine if this boy was saved like that, too.

So Mikoto spoke:

"I get that there's something really important going on inside you. But do you absolutely have to carry it all yourself? You're half-dead, and you're missing memories! What reason could you possibly have for fighting alone?!"

Kamijou was listening. Mikoto took his silence as a positive and kept going.

"I can fight, too, you know."

She kept going—to fight him squarely and to tell him exactly what she needed to. Everything she couldn't say until now flowed out of her.

"I can help you, too!!"

That wasn't because she was Academy City's third-ranked Level Five, the Railgun. That was insignificant compared to this. Even if she'd lost all her power right that moment and become a Level Zero, she knew beyond a shadow of a doubt that she'd be able to say the same.

"There's no reason you have to keep fighting by yourself!! So say something. Say where you're going, or who you're trying to fight, or something!! Today, I'll fight. I'll make things better for you this time!!"

"Mi...saka..."

"I'll give you a taste of your own medicine! I'll show you how the people who wait for you feel! I'll show you how the people who can't do anything but sleep in a hospital bed and watch from a safe place feel!! That's exactly what you did when you saved the Sisters, wasn't it?! You made me talk to you, and then you went out to face the city's strongest Level Five on your own!! Why don't you apply your logic to yourself once in a while? Why are you the one not asking for anyone's help?!"

As she shouted, she stared directly at Kamijou.

And what she saw there was amazement.

But it was not amazement at how she was talking about things she shouldn't have known. It was the surprise of seeing something he'd kept hidden being forcefully revealed in front of him.

He remembered Accelerator and the Sisters.

On the one hand, she felt relieved. On the other, she hated her own selfishness, for letting such calculated emotion into the picture. She was supposed to be worrying over Kamijou's physical condition right now, not placating her own unease.

Kamijou didn't notice. Or maybe he did, but he let it pass.

"A-anyway, we're going back to the hospital! You won't listen to sense, so I'm not letting you out of my sight until you're back in your room!!" Still grabbing his arm, she called up her map on her cell phone and searched for hospitals.

"...I see..."

For a few moments, Kamijou was flabbergasted, but eventually, he began to slowly move his lips.

It almost looked like a smile.

"You found out..."

Although about ready to collapse, an odd strength returned to him. Mikoto decided that meant he was in the most dangerous state possible, so she didn't let go of his arm.

"But that's not it," he said before Mikoto could get a word in. "I have no memory, so I don't remember the details, but..."

Kamijou's spirit wasn't broken.

"I can't remember myself from before. I can't even imagine what I felt like at the end. But getting beaten up, fighting until even my memories were gone...Not having a reason to keep getting hurt on my own..."

His amnesia had been revealed. That alone should have been a major event. But his true thoughts were somewhere else.

"I think that was probably why I risked my life to the point of losing my memories—so I could say stuff like that."

Mikoto's face froze.

That was the conclusion that lay at the center of Touma Kamijou's mind.

That was why he'd kept the truth of his lost memories a secret—he didn't want to hurt anyone by blaming them or saying something stupid about it.

About a past that he couldn't even remember anymore.

But even then, he had been willing to get hurt to protect something important to him. And he'd actually done it—and this was the result. Not an idealized suicidal wish that would bring tears to your eyes; he'd simply been prepared for the end, for what happened after he did what he needed to do, and he'd pressed on anyway. And this was the result.

"I can't remember what happened a long time ago, but even if I can't, it's thanks to all of it that I'm here now. Whoever I was before, he's moving me now. He's still here—not in my head but in my heart. Even if I don't remember, he knows exactly what I'm trying to accomplish and what I need to do."

Touma Kamijou probably had pride in that, a "something" not even he had any proof existed. His conviction wouldn't allow him regret. If he could have met his past self now, he'd have smiled and said thank you without a moment's hesitation. This boy believed in his fate completely.

"Sorry, Misaka. You should get back soon."

The next thing she knew, her hand had left him. With a strange strength, he had moved his arm away from it.

"I'm going. I can't leave this to someone else. There's nothing forcing me to do it, but…I'm still going. That part will never change. Even if the gears hadn't locked up and I hadn't lost my memories, I'd still need to do the same thing. Touma Kamijou won't let a lack of memories stop him from that."

The boy turned his back to Mikoto and started walking again.

His gait was unsteady; if she'd wanted to go after him, it would have been easy.

What should I do…?

But she couldn't move.

His back was right in front of her. If she reached out, she could touch him.

I didn't say anything wrong. He needs to go back to the hospital right now. And I could always go with him to the battlefield…But I know he's not lying. Him standing here, now, like this, on his own feet, must have a special meaning for him.

As she thought, Kamijou moved.

As she worried, he walked away.

But I can't stop him after that. How could I? Seeing him off now is the right choice. Putting my hands together, praying to God, and hoping he comes home safe is the best option. Any other choice, no matter what it is, would be too much. I know he doesn't want that...

His unsteady back grew distant. She had no time left.

She knew she needed to stop him, but she just couldn't move.

What should I do? I can't agree with this at all.

Touma Kamijou probably hadn't lied about anything he'd said. He'd simply revealed his true intentions, still determined to fight merely because he wanted to.

Logically speaking, she should respect that decision and watch over him.

She knew that. Even an idiot would know that.

But she couldn't agree.

She just couldn't.

...I...see.

Without knowing it, her hand had crept up to her chest.

Mikoto Misaka had realized something.

She had an opinion at her core—one not related to logic, reason, reputation, appearances, shame, or scandal. *That* was at the very heart of who she was. She was wretched, ugly, selfish, and whining—but she realized it made her a thoroughly honest, open *human*.

She didn't know what this emotion was called.

She didn't yet understand how to categorize it.

But today, on this day, at this hour, at this moment...

...she understood a certain thing.

She knew there was an immense emotion sleeping inside her, one strong enough to easily ruin outward appearances. As one of only seven Level Fives in the city, she was fully used to controlling her own mind in the form of her personal reality. But this emotion could easily shatter all that.

Touma Kamijou's back disappeared into the dark.

The end had come, and she couldn't stop him.

It wasn't because his movements had touched her.

It was this glimpse of an emotion she'd accidentally found inside herself, not letting her move a finger.

2

Acqua of the Back's mace rumbled.

Not from a special spell or Soul Arm. It was pure physical strength. The difference between Kanzaki, who used her special spell Single Glint for a temporary boost in power, and Acqua, who kept running at sky-high full power, suddenly widened—and then came to its limit.

There was a thundering *thump!!*

Kaori Kanzaki, along with the Seven Heavens Sword she'd used to parry the mace, went flying.

"Gaaaaaaahhhhhhhhhhhhhhh?!"

Kanzaki, whose fight was crushing the heap of rubble under her feet, shot almost a hundred meters through the air. It was like her body had become a cannonball—she blew through one piece of debris after another, crushed concrete chunks to pieces, and scattered their dust all about.

"Over already, saint of the Far East?"

Disappointment filled Acqua's voice.

But Kanzaki, stopped under a mountain of debris, didn't have enough strength to reply. The strength in her bloody body was half what she'd started with, maybe less.

There...must be...

There were no tricks or traps. It was a fundamental difference in skill. So what way could she find to stop him?

What is...his power...?

As she hacked up another clot of blood, she came to a question.

She understood something, as someone who could output the full power of a saint via her Single Glint. Being a saint meant you were already beyond physical human limitations. From the start, that spell had been an instant-kill sword-drawing technique—because if she used it any differently, it could lead to destruction of her own body.

Acqua was past all that.

That was why this difference between them had formed.

There's nothing...extra...in Single Glint's composition...

Her spell didn't just increase momentum. It was built to push a human body to the limit but not destroy their muscles. It was built to move at extreme speeds but not at the cost of balance. All of it was built like a delicate jigsaw puzzle—a pure crystallization of technique. If she demanded more, if she tried to add more pieces to the puzzle, the spell's entire balance would fall apart. You can't add extra pieces to a jigsaw puzzle that is already complete.

This was the limitation of a saint mainly fighting in close quarters.

Did that mean Acqua had created a spell to control his physical body that was more polished than that?

Kanzaki had tried several hypotheses, but they'd all failed.

Every time, if she pushed her abilities in one area, it exhausted another part of herself too much. The moment she came out with abilities on Acqua's level, her body would break apart like a damaged airplane. Both physically *and* magically.

But Acqua...His power...

To begin with, a saint couldn't even exhibit 100 percent of the power they were given.

It was said being born with similar physical characteristics to the Son of God allowed them to graciously acquire a fraction of his strength. But even a fraction was something a regular human couldn't fully grasp.

They could only control an even tinier part of that fraction.

That was how saints were.

No matter how one put together a spell, something would always be too much. In blunt terms, all that power you were given would dissipate. Unlike the power entering your body because of idol worship theory, you could only control so much of it with your own will.

But it wasn't a bad thing that it was too much. If you could use 100 percent of the power, you instead ran the risk of putting so much pressure on yourself that you'd blow your saintly body to bits. That, perhaps, was more of a self-preservation instinct than anything related to sorcery—because the one thing a baby without any magical knowledge knew how to do was stabilize their own power.

But…

…The limit of a saint…doesn't apply…to Acqua…? His power…is already easily…beyond what a human can control…?

This was saying nothing of Acqua's powers as part of God's Right Seat overlapping his sainthood. He was called Acqua of the Back—and thus possessed the attributes of the archangel Gabriel, the "Power" of God. At a glance, it might seem like it was simply multiplying his strength, but in actuality, the burden that would bounce back would have to increase, too.

Yes.

The oddest thing was that Acqua had a grasp of easily over 200 percent power, and not only was it not going out of control—but he'd maintained a steady face the entire time.

…There's no…way he can do that. It has nothing to do with talent or genius. A saint…and God's Right Seat. There should be no way a single body could hold these incompatible traits inside it at once…

The term *genius* had a lot of persuasive power behind it, enough to convince someone most anything was possible.

But it wasn't, really.

Kanzaki was in that realm herself, and she knew.

The terms *genius* and *talent* weren't so convenient in reality.

…Something's…going on…

She heard a soft *tap*. It was Acqua of the Back, coming to a stop in front of her.

…A saint…and God's Right Seat…

Kanzaki thought, glaring at the terrible enemy before her.

…He has to be using some kind of trick to make those two powers coexist…!!

"!!"

Before Acqua took another step, Kanzaki, still lying on the ground, rolled to the side.

She snatched up the Seven Heavens Sword from the ground.

At the same time, Acqua whirled his five-meter-plus mace horizontally. As if to brush away all the debris along with the ground itself—a pure brute-force strike.

Kanzaki's katana, which had aimed for a surprise attack, needed to switch to defense.

Mace and katana clashed with a tremendous *keeeeen!!* The second blow from the mace nearly sent her flying again, but she stabbed her katana into the ground to stop herself—and then still slid over ten meters back.

"You would continue to fight?"

Acqua sounded impressed.

But it was the kind of "impressed" one got after realizing they had the upper hand.

"You will have no chance to turn this around. You should understand this, given your own hand and the number of cards in mine. If miracles occurred in response to endeavors and prayers, then the few saints like ourselves would not be lionized."

"...We're...lionized, are we?" murmured the wound-covered Kanzaki. She sounded disgusted, all the way from the deepest pits of her self. "You didn't work for this power. It was an option that was attached to you from the day you were born. Are you satisfied wielding something easy?"

"What would you do if I answered?" Acqua didn't give her a reply. "I believe we talked about this before—about how much truth lies in convictions you want others to hear."

Kanzaki and Acqua jumped at the same time.

They clashed head-on, sparks flying between metal and metal.

"I know what enrages you. Normal humans, the Amakusa, they all have an overwhelming lack of ability compared to me. You are mad that I involved them in a fight between saints."

"...!!"

"This, however, is a battlefield. Difference in inborn abilities, the strengths of the weapons you possess, and the number of combat personnel. These are clear differences that attack you on a battlefield. If you would rather me not involve them, they should not have come *here* to begin with."

This was no longer a close contest.

Kanzaki buckled under Acqua's power, and she withdrew.

"I have no need to fight those without strength," said Acqua as Kanzaki tottered unsteadily. "I would rather cross blades only with true soldiers."

Was that a glimpse of Acqua's unspoken conviction?

Unlike the others in God's Right Seat, this man told them he would destroy only the boy's right arm.

Was this a fragment of his heart, the heart of someone who purposely wielded the power of Mary, the power of mercy, rather than that of an angel?

Kanzaki's feelings were of a similar philosophy.

Battlefields were all too unmerciful, and pure combat strength, to say nothing of how much one had trained, had no meaning. No matter how much you prepared, you would die when it came time to die. If a saint like her hated that, the only thing she could do was go around and eliminate all the scattered risks in advance, then force a fight on a safe battlefield.

But obviously, that wasn't possible.

If you just had to consider respective combat strength and the possibility of soldiers lying in ambush, maybe it would be possible. But actual battlefields didn't work that way. It was impossible to grasp every single possible nightmarish coincidence in advance and impossible to successfully prevent them all.

Kanzaki had seen this as a sign of her own inexperience.

She wasn't strong enough, which was why she couldn't control the battle, always changing as it was, and her precious friends had been hurt. That was what she'd truly felt *back then*. At the time, Kanzaki, their Priestess, couldn't bear it and ended up breaking ties with the Amakusa.

However…

What…

Kaori Kanzaki, seeing herself in Acqua of the Back, grated her teeth.

What an arrogant way of thinking.

Amakusa's sorcerers had been weak, so they had died—if they had powers like a saint, everybody would have lived. But was that true? How *could* it be true? If it was, then what about the boy? What about the boy who fought alongside everyone, won alongside everyone, and laughed alongside everyone?

She'd said she would fight with them—but had she ever really *believed* in the Amakusa-Style Crossist Church's abilities? Not in their character, or their minds, but their abilities? Wasn't that why Kanzaki couldn't entrust her back to anyone? Wasn't that why coordination had broken down? Wasn't that why she'd been doing nothing but piling on losses they didn't need?

Was the Amakusa-Style Crossist Church that weak?

Which one of them had *really* been the weak one?

What could she possibly gain by forcing a win in her terrible state?

If the ages had moved in the way everyone wanted them to, if the world had moved in a better direction, could those who never gained the strength to win be able to keep up with it?

They would think they'd been left behind.

They would think they'd been left out, alone, from the shining light of happiness filling everything.

A saint.

All they had was what they were born with. Fools, wielding their privilege as "chosen ones." How far did this clash of fools have to go before she was satisfied?

"I'm…a huge idiot," she mumbled in disgust.

She'd witnessed all the unconscious violence she'd committed before now.

That's what this was all about.

Acqua of the Back, God's Right Seat, and Kaori Kanzaki were all the same.

Let someone "special" manage everything. For everything else, simply say the word, and she will manage it for you. It's for your own sake. Putting in pointless effort would make you look miserable, waste our limited resources, and make you a laughingstock—so don't do anything. Just be quiet and obey. At some point, had Kanzaki, without knowing it, begun demanding that of her precious friends?

"…"

Kaori Kanzaki wiped the blood off her lip and readied her sword once more.

Which was the right choice?

I know which one.

What was truly the right choice to save her friends?

I know which one!

Which choice was suitable for correcting the mistakes of this absolute enemy, Acqua of the Back?

I know which one!!

Having solved one thing, the rest began to unravel in a chain of revelation. Her hands tightened around the Seven Heavens Sword. Her final strength. The strength of her conviction, which she could put on full display, because she could believe it was correct.

Acqua of the Back, who wielded the powers of both a saint and a part of God's Right Seat.

With the strongest opponent she'd ever faced before her eyes, Kaori Kanzaki began her final action.

3

At that same moment, the current members of Amakusa, who were staring down in a trance from the edge of the fourth stratum's new crater—about thirty meters above the fifth stratum where the two saints fought, give or take—heard her words.

"……er."

The voice of a true saint, one of less than twenty in the world.

"Please…"

The voice of their Priestess, who had once led Amakusa.

"Please lend me your strength!!"

The voice of Kaori Kanzaki.

At first, Itsuwa, Tatemiya, and the others didn't understand what she'd said. Their brains had processed the intent behind her words, but it didn't seem like it was directed at them.

But no—she *was* speaking to them.

Kaori Kanzaki, whom they thought they'd never reach. Kaori Kanzaki, whom they thought was different from birth, someone with more than them. Kaori Kanzaki, who had turned her back on their weakness, saying she didn't want her precious friends to be hurt.

She was asking for their help.

Their help, to defeat an enemy she couldn't defeat alone.

"...Ah..."

How many realized they were trembling, then?

How many realized they were about to break into tears?

What Kaori Kanzaki had meant by her words and actions was this:

Their Priestess had accepted them.

Accepted them not as simple burdens, comrades-in-arms—but as real friends who stood as her equals in strength.

She'd never done anything like this before.

Why had Kaori Kanzaki requested the Amakusa-Style Crossist Church's help at this point in the game?

It was simple.

There was an enemy here that Kaori Kanzaki couldn't beat on her own.

But she had a reason to confront him despite that.

And...

...her hope to accomplish it in spite of impossibility...

...the final piece she needed to protect her dream...

...was the awfully, terribly normal Amakusa-Style Crossist Church, complete with Tatemiya, Itsuwa, and all the others.

"..."

How long had they been waiting for it? This moment?

Those who had dropped their weapons in enervation now picked them up again.

No one would refuse her.

They were wrapped in bandages, blood seeping from their wounds, the protective fabric itself ripped and torn—but none of that mattered.

They were going to confront this monster—who they couldn't beat as a group, who even Kaori Kanzaki couldn't hold a candle to—but not a single heart had fear at her voice telling them to rise again. Instead, happiness had a greater hold.

They could help their Priestess. They could fight alongside her again. That simple fact gave birth to joy.

Some let out roars to rally their fighting spirit. Others shed the brightest tears in the world. Some stood silently, basking in the happiness, trying not to let anyone see. Those leaning against the wall rose back to their own two feet. Tatemiya, the "representative" pope, exhaled, as though a heavy burden had suddenly been lifted.

"...Let's go."

Saiji Tatemiya, as the temporary leader of the Amakusa-Style Crossist Church, gave the final order.

As if those two words weren't enough, he spoke again, this time with a thousand emotions behind his words.

"Let's go! Our Amakusa-Style Crossist Church now goes to where it needs to be!!"

With a shout, they raced down through the giant hole in the fourth stratum, descending onto the battlefield.

They knew full well how much power they lacked.

But that didn't shake the reason they had to fight.

The Amakusa-Style Crossist Church, as a group, confronted their enemy.

With the lone woman they'd recognized as their leader.

4

What...?

Acqua of the Back didn't understand Kaori Kanzaki's act.

It was clearer than a blazing fire what would happen if she dragged normal sorcerers onto a battlefield of saints. In fact, Kanzaki had distanced Acqua from them because she didn't want that, because she wanted specifically to create a battleground for them alone.

And yet, now…

"Oooohhhhhhhh!!"

One ran past holding a sword, and another jumped high with a spear. Those who didn't fear death assembled in the blink of an eye, forming a battle line to protect their gravely wounded saint.

It was a wall fragile as candy, from Acqua's point of view.

He readied his mace and made a dangerous expression. "Asking for weaklings to save you…Do you value your life that much?"

"Is that what it looks like?" replied Kaori Kanzaki, bringing her Seven Heavens Sword around with bloodied hands.

In fact, there was a smile on her lips.

"I once had comrades who were hurt because they were at my side. I feared it would happen again, so I decided to leave the Amakusa-Style Crossist Church for a time.

"But," she said firmly, "that tragedy didn't happen because they were weak."

"…"

"I labeled them weak, unable to bring myself to have faith in their abilities. Somewhere in my mind, I looked down on them, unable to entrust them with my life. I abandoned the strength right next to me, fighting on despite my inexperience, and in so doing, showed my enemies a glaring weakness! My arrogance, my sense of superiority in thinking I would protect them, was the root of all that tragedy!!"

Those aware of their weaknesses grow when they advance in spite of them.

A new power swirled within Kaori Kanzaki's beaten flesh.

"I will surmount this. I will take back my Amakusa-Style Crossist Church by believing in them, trusting them, and letting them all display their full power!! *We* are our leader, and *we* are our comrades!! We have no need of a single person like a saint to lead us!!"

What…?

He could tell that she'd regained the confidence she'd been lacking.

It was heart.

A stubborn, firm passion that only those with confidence in their own actions possessed.

But it didn't change the fact that they had no chance at victory. Fifty more added to the rabble meant nothing. He didn't need his full power to fight Amakusa as it was now. They were people in the background, ones who would be blown away during his heated combat with Kanzaki.

They cling to impossible illusions—group psychology at work.

"Groundless hopes are naught but delusion."

Power filled Acqua's body.

"You think you can surpass me with delusion?!"

He swung his mace, annoyed, as though swatting pests out of the way. Kaori Kanzaki lunged into range without fear.

The Seven Heavens Sword and his mace collided, but several Amakusa members developed defensive magic to kill the impact. Whatever spiritualism they brought wouldn't change the difference in their abilities. And yet, after all that, Kanzaki contended.

"Saints were born with physical characteristics very similar to the Son of God, and by idol theory, they have received a temporary fragment of his power."

By her own admittance, there had been a blank space of several years between Kanzaki and the Amakusa.

But the two forces didn't even trade words. They overcame all that time in the span of a breath.

"But even a saint cannot use as much power as you. You clearly have powers above those of a simple saint. And why is that?"

Their contention was a sham.

Acqua immediately counterattacked, sending a major wave through Amakusa's ranks, including Kanzaki.

Yet the Amakusa-Style Crossist Church still fought in desperation.

"The answer is simple—the Adoration of Mary!!"

Yes, come to think of it, Acqua had been forthright with them in that. He'd told them he used the attribute of Mary.

But the power Acqua of the Back should have had was that of the

archangel Gabriel, God's "Power." Compared to the Virgin Mother, a symbol of mercy, Gabriel had burned the entire city of Gomorrah, and in the legends, he would deliver even more direct attacks during the Last Judgment to destroy the world. Why had Acqua avoided such an obvious method of attack and instead chosen the roundabout way of Mary?

"Your physical characteristics resemble more than the Son of God, don't they? They're similar both to Jesus and to Mary, which is why you obtained both their powers!!"

The Son of God and the Virgin Mary were mother and child. Their physical characteristics being similar to one another wasn't that surprising a fact.

And Mary, too, number two in Crossism after Jesus, was said to be the highest of the saints, having great powers as the being who had miraculously given birth to the Son of God. The Adoration of Mary, which extolled her, had moved an incredible number of hearts. As one who had granted exceptional mercy, even more than the impartial Jesus—who was himself an embodiment of the very rules of the world—churches had reports of many miracles occurring by praying to her. At times, the Roman Orthodox Church leaders had even viewed the adoration of Mary with danger, worried that Marian worship could become an independent faction.

A saint and the Holy Mother.

If someone had been born with physical characteristics of both of them…

…it would create Acqua of the Back.

He had probably perfected his talents, given to him at birth, by improving them as God's Right Seat.

How deep did the power within him run?

"You were born with two differing qualities and, at the same time, two sets of physical characteristics that overlapped. That is why my gifts alone lost in power to yours, as I am *only* a saint."

To begin with, God's Right Seat was a term for those above humans, those who aimed for the *kami-jou*, a "God above." Their goal had never been to be simple saints.

Because Kanzaki herself was a "mere" saint, it would be very difficult for her to envision such territory. But the "certain power" that saints and angels possessed had the trait of stabilizing once a certain line was crossed. Airplanes were easier to control if they were slower, but too slow and they would fall. Acqua was purposely flying that plane at very high speeds, thus stabilizing it.

It was above a spacious emptiness from a saint's perspective, that line where high speeds stabilized.

By possessing the qualities of both a saint and Mary, he was born with that stabilization line, which was unlike normal saints, who would lower their speed to try to stabilize their power. That was doubtlessly why he'd succeeded in forcing all that power, which would have been unstable and out of control, to come together.

However…

"On the other hand, that means you have a weakness," said Kaori Kanzaki.

Yes—for planes flying at Mach speeds were obviously harder to manage, their control more delicate, than planes taking it slow.

"You must have even more of a weakness than I do, than any saint—to spells that specifically target them!"

Kanzaki stopped talking.

To talk to someone else.

Not Acqua but her Amakusa comrades.

In other words…

"The Saintbreaker!!"

"!"

"Acqua parried all your attacks or dodged them—*but that spell was the only one where he used a magical method for a genuine defense.* That is where our chance at victory lies!!"

Normal humans couldn't completely control saintly power, much less use both it and God's Right Seat at the same time. Kanzaki was a saint herself, so she knew that already.

At first, she thought there was some special spell he was using to perfectly control his power.

She never found out what it was—but of course she didn't.

He didn't have one at all.

"What would happen if we used the Saintbreaker, which has never been tested, and hit Acqua, another exceptional being, with it? Even he couldn't imagine it!!"

Acqua hadn't used his full power to block the Saintbreaker just because it would render a fraction of his stocked power unusable for a few seconds.

"The Saintbreaker purposely upsets the balance of his Jesus-like physical characteristics, causing the power inside to run rampant, which disables the saint for a time. Normally, it would only silence him for a few seconds, but Acqua has characteristics of both a saint and Mary. The end is clear for all to see—he would detonate!!"

The spell he used depended on delicate inborn traits more than sainthood.

In other words, he couldn't strengthen it through artificial methods.

If that godlike balance was thrown off even slightly, everything could go up at that moment. It was like a drag on a machine that could hit at over a thousand kilometers per hour. Because it handled immense force, you needed careful attention. That was why Acqua had used his "full power" to go on the defensive.

"..."

With his mystery solved, Acqua didn't say a word.

But his face did change.

A grin.

Not the condescending sort before now. He'd been named perfect, but there was a single pinhole. They'd pointed it out—and that made the man, Acqua, give a grand smile.

He wouldn't panic over a weakness.

That wasn't what battles were about.

He launched into another series of fierce attacks. Kanzaki barely managed to stop them with her Seven Heavens Sword, exhaling just a bit. Then she slightly changed her sword's angle, purposely causing a shock wave from her strike's aftermath.

It wasn't aimed at Acqua. Instead, it destroyed something behind him.

Part of the scenery, buried under heaps of rubble—a rusted piece of barbed wire.

...I see. That's what they're after...?!

By the time Acqua looked up, the sharp wires, cut to shreds and launched into the air, had just formed a circle. Following that, Kanzaki's wires, the Seven Glints, sliced through their surroundings once again. Magical meanings abstracted one after another from the pile of debris, coming up like carvings.

What appeared was a giant cross, a spike like a sharp steel pile, and a crown of thorns.

In other words...

"Symbols of Jesus's crucifixion!!" he shouted.

Anyone wielding a fraction of Jesus's power as a saint inherited his weaknesses, too.

Still, if rubbish like this could defeat a saint, nobody would have trouble.

In fact, against a normal saint like Kanzaki, it wouldn't do much.

But...

Acqua of the Back was a *special* saint.

Someone with even rarer physical characteristics than the other saints in the world. One who simultaneously wielded the powers of saints and the Holy Mother. In exchange for that immense power, he needed to have incredibly delicate control. That was why the symbols of the crucifixion Kaori Kanzaki formed in this place alone would have an effect.

One might think a crucifixion spell wouldn't have anything to do with Mary, but in this case, that wasn't correct.

Yes—for Mary was also considered the highest Crossist saint in all of history.

"...!!"

Kanzaki sensed something bubbling up inside Acqua's physics-defying body.

A change so clear even an ordinary saint could see it.

In other words, Acqua of the Back...

"...He's wavering," stated Kanzaki confidently.

The powers of saint and Holy Mother overlapped each other at the central core of Acqua's existence. Now, under pressure from an outside source, they were competing, sending up harsh, screeching cries.

Right now, they could do it.

So Kaori Kanzaki bellowed, "Preparations are complete! Longinus, grant us the final key to the rite of crucifixion!!"

"!!"

Itsuwa, who gripped the Saintbreaker's key, understood Kanzaki's words. She immediately took out a hand towel, then wrapped it around her Friulian spear before leveling it at him.

"...Interesting."

But Acqua moved first.

"The Amakusa-Style Crossist Church, was it? I dub thy name worthy of remembrance!!"

Then he jumped twenty meters—no, over twice that, all the way through the crater connecting the fourth and fifth stratum. As he went, dozens, hundreds of wires danced through the night sky, but none of them could stop him.

The city lights filtering through the circular crater made it look like a giant moon.

And with that artificial moon behind him, he readied his mace.

"The Holy Mother mitigates severe punishment."

Before, this attack had crashed down on Kaori Kanzaki with all the destructive force of an asteroid collision. Enough power to crush her even at full strength. On top of that, the power would easily double due to the height of his jump. Amakusa couldn't possibly stand up to it as they were now. It would destroy this entire fifth stratum.

"This power, which at times appeals directly to God's law. Let it wrap you in mercy and ascend to heaven!!"

With immense speed, Acqua shot downward. His mace, bathed in the nightscape's light, left a bluish-white trail in its wake.

No!! thought Kanzaki, building a defensive line with all the wires she'd positioned in advance, trying to stop the iron hammer. But it wasn't enough. His strike blew through it and continued to approach the ground.

This attack had hit Kanzaki directly, so she knew: If she was hit by another, she would die. Not only her but the rest of the nearby Amakusa members, too.

The safety net…!!

As Kanzaki gritted her teeth in frustration, Itsuwa aimed her spear overhead.

The Saintbreaker.

But the preparations for the spell weren't finished yet. They wouldn't make it.

Give up…

Kaori Kanzaki reached for her sword.

Acqua descended like a wave of pure destruction. She looked up, glaring, pressing her feet hard into the debris-laden plaza. In a flash, she drew the katana, positioning it horizontally.

It wasn't for a counterattack.

Everything was for defense. She immediately drew every mark, every sign, every symbol from every time and place in her mind to build a spell to serve as a shield.

I won't give up!!

Acqua of the Back fell to the ground with all his might.

Light raged.

Kaori Kanzaki's eyes, her ears, her nose, her tongue, her skin—all of it disappeared.

5

Destruction.

She couldn't even understand that one word.

Her five senses were dead. The world was white. Nothing made it to her brain. Not the raging shock waves, not the whipping dust, not the smell of metal, not the sensation of being crushed. Was this how far destruction needed to go to be true—to be pure annihilation?

"…"

She needed time for her whited-out senses to return.
Then Kanzaki realized something.
Little by little, her senses were returning.
They hadn't been lost. They were recovering, which meant…
What…?
Acqua of the Back's attack should have destroyed everything in its path. It should have taken the lives of all the Amakusa, including her, with change left over. Kanzaki, however, was unharmed, as though his spell had disappeared. There was no damage anywhere that she could see.
It's…gone…? The spell, the magic—it's gone?
Kanzaki came to and looked up.
One act, in disregard of good or evil, strong or weak, that would cancel any sorcery without an issue.
She knew of only one person who could do something so absurd.
"Could it…be…?"
Her senses returned.
Her own words made it to her ears, and it was as though it signaled the rest of her senses to breathe back into her. Despite Acqua's nightmarish strike, the scenery was the same as before, as though literally *nothing had happened.* And one person stood at the center of it.

Touma Kamijou.
He suppressed Acqua's magical attack head-on, then grabbed the mace hard enough to crush it.

If Acqua of the Back had swung his mace with purely physical strength, the blood-covered Kamijou's right hand would have been crushed to pieces. But this was a purely magic-based attack. And his right hand had the ability to blow away any supernatural powers, no matter what they were.
Even if Acqua's attack had been an extremely powerful spell.
His right hand brutally nullified it all!!
"What…?!!"

"..."

The bloody Kamijou murmured something to the shocked Acqua. Nobody else heard it. And then Kamijou collapsed, leaning up against the mace. He hadn't run out of energy—he was trying to stop Acqua from moving.

"!!"

Seeing that, Kanzaki moved.

On his own, Kamijou would be knocked away with a flick of the mace. But she used Acqua's momentary shock to her advantage, discarding the Seven Heavens Sword and grabbing Acqua's shoulders as though she were gripping a log, trying to stop both him and the mace from moving.

"Bastards!!"

Acqua shouted something, but the two of them weren't listening.

The wound-covered Kamijou and Kanzaki were looking at the same place.

To Itsuwa, of the Amakusa-Style Crossist Church.

To Itsuwa, just a regular sorcerer.

"Please, leave this to me..."

Itsuwa readied her spear again, grabbing its shaft with her hand towel, as the other Amakusa members started up their own unique spells.

"I will hit this time!!"

With a roar, Itsuwa launched.

The girl's slender body, under the protection of several spells, accelerated at Acqua.

He tried to evade her.

But his saintlike physical force was sealed away by another saint, Kanzaki, and when he triggered a special Mary spell to drive her away as God's Right Seat, Kamijou's right hand blew it all away.

"Ohh..."

He was only incapacitated for a few short seconds.

But that was all they needed.

"...ooohhhhhhhhhhhhhhhhhhhhhhhhhhhhhhhhh!!"

At that moment, Acqua gave a war cry.

It wasn't out of terror.

He realized he wouldn't be able to dodge the next attack, but his conviction wouldn't waver. In fact, the battle shout had been to give him extra force so he could take a big step forward, toward the charging Itsuwa.

The Saintbreaker.

Itsuwa's spear split apart, turning into a single bolt of lightning. Free from its physical restraints, it became a strike that dominated the space, bursting toward Acqua.

Ba-boom!! The noise rattled the very air.

The flash of lightning struck Acqua in the gut, then escaped out his back, this time penetrating into his entire body.

The impact from the hit caused Kamijou and Kanzaki to pull back.

A cross—of light, not sparks—burst out behind Acqua, vertically and horizontally. However, Acqua's body, which had taken the hit, leaped straight into the center of that cross, where the lines intersected.

His body, having received the Saintbreaker, careened over meters of concrete tile. The giant mace left his hands, and he soared away, plunging into one of the fifth stratum's man-made ponds. As he shot under the surface like a cannonball and went out of sight, another change occurred.

Mana went out of control.

Acqua of the Back had detonated.

When his attributes of saint and Mary suffered the Saintbreaker, they reacted, began to compete, and then caused a rapid chain of internal explosions the spell would never have been able to cause otherwise.

Kap!! A flash of light engulfed the midnight-dark pond, illuminating it as though it were midday. The flash momentarily blinded everyone, but they still heard the eerie noise of large amounts of water vaporizing all at once.

When Kaori Kanzaki opened her eyes again, Acqua was no longer there.

But all the water in that man-made pond had evaporated. It had been blown away, along with the pond's edge. A pillar of water vapor, the same thickness as the pond itself, rose straight up. The giant column collided with the ceiling section of the underground city, then dispersed in every direction. The sight was overwhelming, like a giant tree that had lived for over a thousand years, belying the incredible force of Acqua's abrupt detonation.

INTERLUDE FOUR

About ten years ago, in a deserted port.

William Orwell rubbed his punched cheek.

The Knight Leader was the one who'd struck him.

Between the discontented pair was the Third Princess of Britain, who had been labeled incompetent by the world. Of course, that was why it hadn't been a problem for her to sneak out of the castle like this.

"That was for lying to me and taking all the good parts for yourself."

The Knight Leader cracked his knuckles, approaching William with an expression he'd never let society see.

"I'm not done. I haven't punched you for leaving England yet. So let me make sure. We can't have any mistakes happening. Here's my question. Do you really plan on leaving England?"

"Yes."

As soon as William answered, the Knight Leader punched him hard in the face again. *Thump!!* Meanwhile, the third princess yelped and covered her face.

William's face was actually the calmest of them all, despite the beating. "…Are you drunk?" he asked.

"If I was, I'd be hitting you with the empty bottle." The Knight

Leader dropped the leather rucksack and fished around in it. "I've got some good scotch. First-rate, without a drop of caramel. Pure barrel color. Yeah, it's full, but don't worry about it. You're leaving today, after all. I'm giving you such a big present that I think I have the right to punch you."

"What are you angry about anyway?" asked William.

The Knight Leader paused, then eventually said, "You'll be more than just a mercenary."

"Have you ever heard the word *overestimation*? No, you probably haven't."

"I worked so hard to get them to finally accept you as a knight in your own right, too...Talk about ruining someone's efforts. You planning on becoming a great artist somewhere, then? You have to be insane to choose a life people will only acknowledge hundreds of years from now."

"I don't know a thing about art. Nor of the lives of those who create it."

"...What is your goal? You must have a good reason for turning down this invitation."

"It is not as though I wish to do anything special," answered William casually. "As I said before, knights and mercenaries do not mix. Knights in this country have great authority, but that isn't enough to solve some problems. The same goes for mercenaries. I may be free to roam, but I am finding it quite difficult to enter into the realm of *trust*."

"...You..."

"I need to have both, as I am sure this incident has taught you. There are problems a swollen group alone cannot resolve. That brings into necessity observation from an outside source. That observer cannot be special alone, either. The cogs forming society may come in different sizes, but everyone influences them and turns them together. This is a truth that must not be forgotten."

William was correct, and the Knight Leader knew his personality, so he fell silent, expression morose. Seeing his old friend make that face put a subtle smile on William's lips.

"I am also concerned," said William, "about why the royal family's faction is trying to expand its sphere of influence through drastic measures. You know the United Kingdom is made up of three factions—the royal family, the Knights, and the Puritans. The royal family is easily influenced by the Puritans. I believe it correct to assume something happened there."

The Knight Leader appeared to think of the Puritans' leader. The Archbishop—Laura Stuart.

With her position as top of one of the three factions, she was in an equivalent position to the Knight Leader. This knight probably didn't appreciate that fact, though. She was just that ominous a person.

William continued. "The problems extend outside the United Kingdom's borders. Roman Orthodoxy, Russian Catholicism, and Academy City are all showing unsettling movements. The world is trying to change. And such change causes organizations to run rampant."

"As a member of the Knights' faction, I would think we also have the option of stabilizing England."

"I do not believe that would solve everything on its own. This incident was a good example. I choose to protect from the outside. You need to protect from the inside. If we do this, the breadth of our choices will expand. It increases the probability that one of us can be stopped if we do go out of control."

"No point debating this anymore, then," said the Knight Leader in a lonely tone. Then, as if to ward that away, he took the bottle of scotch from his sack and pushed it at William. "A parting gift. Chamberlain even said this was his best stuff this year."

"...This much would be wasted on one person."

"Then find some good comrades on your travels. Good enough to share it with."

His foppish expression caused William to sigh. They would always be a knight and a mercenary. He was honestly surprised they'd gotten along so well before now.

"Ah yes," said William. "A craftsman should have received an order for an escutcheon. Have him cancel it. If it survives, I feel like my regrets will, too."

Those were the parting words of a mercenary.

No special ceremony or etiquette. The Knight Leader had displayed himself as a land-owning noble, so William responded in the mercenary way, as grass without roots.

When the mercenary left, the Knight Leader muttered to himself.

"...I can't do that."

The third princess looked at him, but he didn't seem to realize he was actually speaking aloud.

"...Damn it, I can't get rid of it like that."

EPILOGUE

Cicerone to Further Disturbance

True_Target_Is…

Touma Kamijou awoke in a hospital bed.

He was used to this room by now. He must have been moved out of District 22 to District 7, where the frog-faced doctor was. Every time he was hospitalized, perhaps because of his link to all these incidents, they took the time to bring him to this single-person room with no other patients. He was actually a little nervous that they might have been seeing him as a massive nuisance.

"Oh, oh—have you woken up?"

That was Itsuwa, who was sitting in a pipe chair set up for a guest visit. Kamijou tried to sit up, but his body wouldn't move. And it wasn't just his deep wounds doing the talking there; he felt a strange sense of exhaustion—he had no energy at all. It felt like the core of his tiredness was spread throughout his whole body. As he wondered in confusion about this unaccustomed sensation, Itsuwa sighed in relief and relaxed.

"I-it's only natural you can't move. You slipped out of the hospital when you were supposed to have absolute bed rest and went back to the battlefield, and then you pulled off a surprise attack against Acqua."

He asked Itsuwa a few things—after they'd fought off Acqua of the Back, no civilians or Amakusa members had died. But it didn't feel real at all.

Actually, he couldn't remember much of what had happened after sneaking out. He felt like he'd run into Mikoto on the way, but how much of that had been a dream? Still, he was fundamentally hiding the fact that he was an amnesiac, so he wouldn't talk much about not remembering parts of events. For now, he smiled vaguely.

"...Still, well...That was crazy. Acqua was God's Right Seat and a saint at the same time, right? And you beat him...Does that mean I witnessed a historical moment?

"Y-you were the one who did the most! In fact, it was a miracle we even beat a saint, and on top of that, we did it without any losses—it's like Santa Claus tripped and all the presents came out of his bag at once and flew all over the game board, and...!!"

For some reason, Itsuwa went red in the face and started waving her arms in front of her surprisingly large chest...Well, anyway, the takeaway was that Amakusa was amazing for beating him, right? It was a super-sloppy judgment, since Kamijou didn't know anything about the world of sorcery.

Though in reality, it had actually been Itsuwa holding the key—the Saintbreaker—who had delivered the finishing blow, but she didn't seem to realize that whatsoever. Which was worse: a natural, air-headed idiot or a serious, humble one? Anyway, he could sum it up as incredibly unfair from Acqua's point of view.

"Blah...Wait, what day is it? I-I'm still okay on attendance, right?! Crap, I feel like I probably need to make sure of that or something bad will happen!! I feel like incidents have been happening one after another lately!!"

"Oh no, you mustn't get up!!"

Itsuwa grabbed his shoulders and tried to push him back down onto the bed when he tried to get up. As a result, their faces rapidly neared. They were a little less than five centimeters apart. Frankly speaking, Itsuwa's surprised, blushing face had filled his view. He got the sense that the air between their faces had turned into a soft wall, but for some reason, he didn't consider the option of pulling away.

And then...

"....................................Touma, you're the same as always."

Prompted by the low voice, he looked over and saw a girl, in other words, Index, standing idly near the entrance to the hospital room. She came with a bonus: a broken flower vase on the floor at her feet, very nicely expressing her current state of mind. The suspense went off without a hitch, and her timing was perfect—God-given, even, as though he were saying Kamijou would always be dealing with *some* incident.

"E-eeeek!! Wait, *please wait, Miss Index*!! I can tell without you saying it! Your Greatness is about to give up on poor Kamijou's existence and humanity, aren't you?!"

"...I was the one sitting there until a minute ago. I take my eyes off you for one second and it's already gotten to this...You haven't even said sorry for sneaking out of the hospital without telling me..."

"Yes, yes, you're right! I fully agree with that! I wasn't acting sane when I went back to Acqua in that state! What on earth would you have done if the worst had happened?!"

"Acqua?! You mean from God's Right Seat?! *That* Acqua?! How could you not rely on me for an enemy who's basically made of magic?! I'm the Index, for crying out loud!!"

"Wait, what?! When did Itsuwa's position change like that?! Is this the power of Amakusa's environmental adaptation?!"

Meanwhile, in front of the room where their exchange was going on, there was a woman, standing at a loss in the straight hallway: Kaori Kanzaki. She'd come to make her own hospital visit, but it seemed like she'd missed her chance (or been beaten to the punch by Itsuwa), so now she didn't know what to do.

"(...What do I do? I have to go back to London tomorrow, so this is the only chance in my schedule, but both Itsuwa and that child are here at this very moment...)"

"Lady...You're burning daylight, you know."

A sudden voice from right behind her nearly sent her jumping out of her boots. She turned around to find a boy with blond hair and sunglasses—Tsuchimikado Motoharu.

He brought a hand to his mouth and grinned meaningfully. "You've been blessed with a chance to visit Japan in the middle of your very busy schedule. Now's your chance to thank him for taking care of Index and Amakusa, nya."

"I—I know that. But, well...How to put this? Talking to him one-on-one would already be awkward, but now that both Itsuwa and the child are there, well, I'd appreciate waiting a little longer, or, well..."

"Anyway, you brought the fallen angel maid costume, right?"

"*Bfghbt?!* O-of course not!! Why would I?! The Seven Heavens Sword barely got through customs!! Besides, if I was going through with *that* absurd plan, I'd definitely have to get him alone!! I could absolutely not have Itsuwa or that girl in the middle of it!! You know how powerful that girl's eidetic memory is!!"

Kanzaki shook her head quickly, imagining the terrible scene.

But Tsuchimikado, with a know-it-all look, nodded generously. "I know you're super-serious and blush easily, so...Ta-daa!! Today, I brought an evolution of that outfit—an *erotic* fallen angel maid costume, nya!!"

"How is that any different?!"

"Huh? What do you mean? Look, the chest is open more, and the skirt portion is more transparent—"

Kanzaki grabbed onto Tsuchimikado's hand for dear life as he tried to suddenly unfold some kind of fabric in front of her. Despite her saintly gripping force threatening to crush his palm, he maintained a grin, albeit a pained one.

"Then what're you gonna do? Like, seriously, tell me what you're gonna do. You dragged yourself this far—you're not gonna just walk in, smile normally, blush a little, tilt your head, and say thank you, right? You need to realize something! While you've been diddling around, this story's getting to the point where you won't be able to do anything about it!! Don't think I'll let you keep me in all this suspense and then sidestep the entire issue!!"

Fierce lights flew from Tsuchimikado's eyes behind his sunglasses, and Kaori Kanzaki lost all her usual coolness. Drawing back, she asked, "Then what do you think I should do?! No matter how much of a debt I accrue, the only thing I can do is wholeheartedly—"

"You can at least give him a squeeze and a rub, damn it!"

"??? Squeeze? Squeeze what?"

"Oh please, get off your freaking high horse...Question, question for you, now!! Zaky, what are *those* attached to your body for? I'm asking you what purpose those proofs of mammal-hood, in other words, those boobs, are stuck to you for!!"

"A-at the very least, they're not for squeezing and rubbing things..."

Kanzaki's face clouded in confusion, unable to imagine what Tsuchimikado was trying to get at.

He clicked his tongue softly. She was being surprisingly hardheaded.

"But really, you're sure you're all right with going at it so slowly, huh?"

"Wh-what are you talking about?"

"(...Look at Itsuwa,)" he whispered. "(You know, the one who's *slow to mature*. I'm telling you, she might be willing to put on the erotic fallen angel getup.)"

"(...???!!! Th-there's no way...!!)" she replied, needlessly drawing in to reflect Tsuchimikado's secretive tone.

He let out a suppressed, catlike grin. "Do you know that for sure? We all tend to think she won't make any bold moves, but considering how much she's going for the hand towel plan, when you really think about it, she acts independently a lot. The towel thing has been doing nothing but failing, so when she comes to terms with what she's missing—the erotic fallen angel maid outfit, I mean—and everything clicks, how much attack power do you think it will give her?"

"Th-that can't be! I know her—she would never do that!!"

"You know, to be blunt, with her size, she'd have no problem squeezing and rubbing."

"??? Again, what do you mean by that?"

Kanzaki gave him another blank look. For once, Tsuchimikado was at his wits' end. He couldn't get her on the same page. He changed his mind, deciding to attack from a different angle.

"In the end, that's all you are, Zaky. The only thing that stands out about you is how embarrassed you get. You don't actually have any gratitude toward Kammy at all, do you?"

"N-no, you're wrong!! It's just that your examples, like that erotic fallen angel maid thing, are too out there!! I'm grateful in a normal way!!"

"But I don't think Itsuwa cares. That means she's more grateful to him than you. To be honest, she could do a simple fallen angel maid outfit, no problem. And she'd want to power it up to the erotic version. Do you know what the difference here is?"

"I—I don't understand what you mean."

"What I mean is, she has you beat, Zaky. On being a woman."

"?!"

"Blech. Is Amakusa even going to be all right like this? Sheesh. Pride's the only thing you've got much of. You don't know what it means to slave away at something. Can you guide little lost lambs like that? When push comes to shove, you'll be the only pretty one left and abandon everyone else, nya."

"N-no, I...This is all too much for a stupid erotic fallen angel maid costume..."

She was 100 percent sure she was in the right, but when he said all this like it was so obvious, she wavered. She already had a debt to Kamijou to begin with. It wasn't taking long for her brain to deflate like a punctured tire.

N-no, this all has to be a ruse! There is no possible way a stupid erotic fallen angel maid costume can determine a woman's worth!! U-um...I feel like that's beside the point...? My worth as a woman isn't the problem; it's how to thank him properly...I keep saying that outfit isn't how, but can I think of any alternatives...? Ack!! I—I mustn't be weak!! This is all a trap!! No, wait, but...Hmm, well...I need to calm down. First, I need to calm down and think this through!!

"Hmm? Wh-what is it, Zaky?"

As her thoughts raced fruitlessly in her mind, Tsuchimikado winced a little. She must not have heard a word he'd said. After putting on a flat, expressionless face, Kanzaki quietly sat down in *seiza* position in the middle of the hospital hallway. Then, with slow movements reminiscent of flower arranging, she took out almost twenty roofing tiles from who knows where and began to pile them up.

"Hhhhnnnnnnnnnnnnnnnnnnnnn!!"

She laid her fist into the pile from above, punching through the tiles and down into the floor. Listening to the breaking, she spoke to Tsuchimikado in an incredibly cool tone of voice.

"I will be fine. I am thinking."

On the other hand, Tsuchimikado, having witnessed an oddly level-faced Priestess, was a little unsure. *Crap. Did I go too far with my half-joking lecture?* He broke into a bit of a cold sweat.

Eventually, Kanzaki held out a swaying hand to him. Her five fingers were in a straight line like for a karate chop, and she had her palm up, pointed at Tsuchimikado as if to take off his head.

She spoke.

"Tsuchimikado."

"Y-yes?"

"I am prepared. The item, if you would."

About ten minutes later...

After burying her fist in the cackling Tsuchimikado's face, withdrawing extra womanliness, and leveling up once again, the Priestess of Amakusa, Kaori Kanzaki, charged into a certain hospital room.

For the sake of the Priestess's honor, we will omit here what sort of chaos struck the world after that.

The one thing we can say is that Touma Kamijou would, for a time afterward, be terrified by the shadow of a third angel, separate from Misha Kreutzev and Hyouka Kazakiri.

A message came from the English Puritan Church.

A person called a strategic negotiator had called to present several documents and several plans for surrender. He'd implied they should choose for themselves the end they wished for most. Before hearing half of it, the pope cut the communication off.

"Damn!!"

He seethed. Acqua losing meant two things. First, they had lost a valuable combat asset. Second, the enemy had more combat potential than they'd thought.

How in the world could Acqua have lost?

Touma Kamijou.

He may have had a rare ability, but that wouldn't beat Acqua alone. However, many people had naturally gathered to defend the boy. His faction—made up of simple friends and comrades.

"…"

The pope of Rome thought in silence.

The boy was formidable.

As he brooded over this with a glower, he heard a set of footsteps.

"This will not do. Acqua, defeated? They must have grown since last time. Still, that's why we have our pretext. Our justice. Hah—should chaos appear in this Roman Orthodox–controlled world, the source must meet with a swift end, no matter who it is, eh?"

Footsteps echoing in the Vatican, within St. Peter's Basilica.

The pope saw him and gave him a deeply troubled look. "Fiamma of the Right…Y-you…You didn't come from *back there*, did you?"

"Well now, isn't that a dangerous look on you?" said the young man, Fiamma, to the pope. He seemed disappointed. "They do say the true stuff of a leader only shows itself in dilemmas. That response just will not do. It makes you look like you aren't worthy of being the pope."

"What…do you plan to do?" asked the pope carefully.

Vento of the Front was recuperating, Terra of the Left had died, and they didn't know if Acqua of the Back was alive. In other words, the one holding decision-making authority for God's Right Seat, and the Roman Orthodox Church, lay in the hands of Fiamma.

Fiamma had always been an ominous presence, even within God's Right Seat. The pope felt as though even the other more self-willed members had always left the final decision on their actions to him.

"Vento's surprise attack on Academy City. Terra's global group control. Acqua's overwhelming genius...Every one of them a failure. Is there a better plan? An overpowering one that will stop Academy City, the main base of the science side?"

The pope's face darkened. The Roman Orthodox pope could not tolerate the science side rising to power—that was why he'd asked instruction from God's Right Seat. Still, he did not want to find himself besieged, with the guiltless faithful caught in the mess.

However, Fiamma said, almost jokingly, the exact opposite of this idea. "First, destroy Britain."

"What?" said the pope.

Fiamma ignored him and continued. "You don't understand? Thanks to our alliance with the Russian Catholic Church, we have complete possession of all Europe aside from them. We contact all the nations and run Britain dry. People, goods, money—we cut off the flow of everything. It is still an island nation, after all. With nowhere to run, I estimate they'll run out of power in a matter of months."

The pope tried once again to understand what Fiamma was saying, but gave up. "I don't understand the point," he said honestly. "True, there is a pipeline between Academy City and the English Puritan Church. But if we take Britain, I don't think that would be a fatal blow to Academy City. Even if we took the entire United Kingdom hostage, that city would be fine with continuing the war. They could use saving them as a pretext, after all."

On the other hand, if they conquered Academy City first, the British side would grind to a halt. English Puritanism may have been one of the three largest denominations of Catholicism, but it also meant they were only one-third of it. They wouldn't start a war against the other two-thirds—the Roman Orthodox and Russian Catholic Churches.

The British were being so aggressive because they were allied with Academy City, and the entire rest of the science side, too. If they could just disable Academy City, Britain would wake up before it was hurt.

"Not quite," interrupted Fiamma simply. "That's not quite right, Mr. Pope of Rome."

"Academy City thinks nothing of us."

This time, the pope caught his breath. He didn't understand what Fiamma of the Right had just said. It wasn't that he half understood—he didn't comprehend a single word.

Fiamma continued, disregarding his shock. "The United Kingdom has something. Something we absolutely need. They won't simply offer it, of course. That was why we had to cause a commotion. To get it, we need the great power of the Roman Orthodox Church to take action."

"What...are you saying...?"

"Hmm? I believe I answered your question. And this isn't necessarily mutually exclusive with *your* wish, either. As long as we get it, we can destroy anything—we could get rid of Academy City and the entire science side at once."

"What...?" The pope still didn't understand. He just asked, "What is that something...?"

"Ah yes."

Fiamma of the Right spoke it easily. And the words he said were...

....

....

There was a *thud*.

It was the sound of the Roman pope staggering and hitting his back against a thick pillar in St. Peter's Basilica.

"That's...absurd...," he managed to say, wringing it from his throat. "Are you truly a Crossist disciple...?"

Fiamma responded casually. "Hmm. Well, what do you think?"

"Damn!!"

"That will not do. You are the pope—swearing like that will simply not do."

The man ignored Fiamma's words of ridicule. He couldn't pay attention to them. Vento of the Front, Terra of the Left, Acqua of the Back. Each of them moved according to his or her own warped principles and ideas, but God's Right Seat was still a single Crossist group. They would acquire powers beyond those of angels, become *kami-jou*, "gods above," and save man directly. While that way of thinking was arrogant and blasphemous, as a person, he could understand parts of it.

But this was different.

Fiamma of the Right, alone, was decidedly different.

He'd told the pope to isolate Britain using the Roman Orthodox and Russian Catholic Churches' power. But Britain wouldn't sit idly by and wait for that to happen. When they realized their energy would actually deplete, they would fight like their lives depended on it. This could turn all of Europe into a battlefield. This was in a different dimension than sending one or two important people sneaking into Academy City—this would cause a genuine war.

"You…You don't think I'll sit quietly and let you do this, I hope."

He couldn't let him do that. He was aware that a conflict had started, one that shouldn't have begun in the first place…but he could still stop it.

"You want to fight?" asked Fiamma, looking directly at him, slowly shaking his head. "Fight the leader of God's Right Seat?"

"Do not look down on me. You are captain of a mud-boat about to sink."

"Strong words. Yes, the others may have had rare *qualities*, but it was just three people. I can just assign the Front, Left, and Back positions to others. As long as I, the great Fiamma, survive."

"You think I'll let you?" rumbled the pope. "Fiamma of the Right. You will be silent for a time. Or perhaps for eternity."

Boom!! An explosion. Nothing in particular had suddenly appeared. Instead, the space itself, unchanging, was wavering, making odd, cracking noises. The scene looked like the inside of a box being crushed from the outside.

"I announce to apostles one through twelve. I beg the Lord who cannot be counted. Power need overflow. I know its proper meaning, and with that power, I desire the defeat of my enemies."

Several lights flew around. They were supposedly mere glowing orbs, but each held within it a completely different image, like a mysteriously upside-down cross and a scallop.

The symbolic lights surrounded Fiamma, forming flat planes between them. A prison shaped like a soccer ball formed around his body.

He heard a whistle.

It came from Fiamma's mouth. Fiamma, who was completely encircled.

"Symbols of Jesus and the twelve apostles? Are you sure? You're even borrowing the seal of Judas, the betrayer. And yet you are the pope."

"Do not misunderstand. Judas may have betrayed the Lord, but it was the Lord's mercy extended to him as an apostle. Thou shalt love thy neighbor. It's easy to bury what works against us. But the purpose of the Word of God is to never seek the easy way out."

Bwoom!! The sound of an explosion.

The thirteen-faced polygon surrounding Fiamma formed a ring to restrain him. Not to physically bind him but to sever his body from his mind and to have them spin fruitlessly within his flesh for eternity—restraints that did not wound.

"After Judas's betrayal, he was overwhelmed by a strong sense of self-reproach and hanged himself. His world was dark, cold, deep, and painful. No matter where he looked, he couldn't even see a single ray of hope. Remember it, for that is what you will experience now."

Fiamma probably couldn't hear him, but the pope kept talking.

"This will force you into a state of idleness for forty years. Have a long taste of the self-isolation Judas succumbed to, and re-polish your inexperienced mind."

Standing frozen inside the thirteen-faced polygon, Fiamma's lips trembled slightly.

Perhaps it was all the resistance he could muster, as he couldn't move a muscle.

"Stop. Despite my failings, I am the pope. The powers I wield now are sacred, ones which have guided and supported two billion faithful for over two thousand years. The arrogance of a single man or two is not enough to ward it away."

In addition, St. Peter's Basilica was the strongest, greatest fortress in the entire Catholic sphere. To top that off, Vatican City itself functioned as one giant Soul Arm, adding layers upon layers of strength to the pope.

"Hmph."

And then Fiamma's mouth actually moved.

Shock entered the pope's expression. Those weren't the movements of someone restrained.

Fiamma spoke, his tone neutral.

"Unfortunately, it was only two billion, and only two thousand years."

A moment later, everything disappeared.

The pope's eyes could just barely make out a brilliant, explosive light from the vicinity of Fiamma's right shoulder. An instant later, his vision had covered over in white, and a storm of destruction had brewed.

A dome-shaped wind blasted.

One-third of St. Peter's Basilica had just been blown to pieces from within.

The magical devices supporting the immense building severed one by one, causing a chain of collapse of other facilities supporting the Vatican, utterly destroying the defensive circle supposedly safeguarding the area, whipping up mana without anywhere to go, bending and warping the scenery.

The pope was blown over a hundred meters back. He rolled onto the cobblestones of a plaza.

He watched, dumbstruck, as the basilica collapsed into dust. The world's strongest fortress, Crossism's largest basilica, tore open like a flimsy piece of paper. The horrible sight made the pope forget even the pain of his wounds.

At the center of all the destruction, Fiamma of the Right reigned supreme.

He slowly began to walk to the plaza.

There was something strange around his right shoulder.

In addition to his arm, there was a distorted bundle of light, like a failed wing, like a giant's arm with five ugly rings on it. Greek mythology spoke of the goddess Athena being born from a wound in Zeus's forehead—and this seemed just as surreal a sight.

"Pathetic. That was all it took for it to break apart?"

Fiamma looked between his right arm and the thing growing out of his shoulder. Then he spat, as though he'd tried to start a car that had a bad engine.

The pope, leaning against broken cobblestones, moaned, "That... arm...Could that be...?"

"Yes. The right arm is the symbol of miracles," said Fiamma, walking slowly into the debris. "Jesus healed the sick with his right hand and raised the dead. We make the sign of the cross with our right hand, and we sprinkle the holy water of baptism with our right hand. And Michael—he who is like God. His right hand held the most powerful weapon in history. It consigned many a fallen angel to oblivion, strong enough to cut down even Lucifer, the bearer of light."

The right.

The man symbolizing the color of burning red, Fiamma, simply continued his lecture.

A lecture to the pope—the highest of the Roman Orthodox Church.

"Urgh..."

"Of course, because this 'holy right,' the right hand of God, has such incredible power, normal humans can't handle it. When regular disciples genuflect or handle holy water, well...you know how the powers those in the legends wield is only a fraction of it? Saints, God's Right Seat, whatever—their flesh is always based on that of a normal human. Do you get it, Mr. Pope? I'm just a regular human. Unfortunately for me," he said, sounding annoyed.

He wielded such inhuman powers at a whim and yet scorned himself as nothing but human.

"What I mean is, I've got this wonderful crystallization of these right-handed miracles but no output terminal for stocking it, controlling it, and exhibiting it. And you barely get anything out of trying to use it like that, right? It's like watching a video taken by a high-definition camera on a monochrome television."

The giant, warped, ominous arm swayed behind Fiamma.

He licked his slender fingers. "Hey, don't you want that power?"

Fiamma of the Right, who had utterly ruined St. Peter's Basilica as though it were no problem, as though it were a mere man-made cathedral, just a few holy secrets assembled as one.

"The Holy Right symbolizes all miracles. The power of the right can destroy any evil or wickedness without issue, bind the Devil himself to the bottom of hell, and guarantee a thousand years of peace. If there were a right arm capable of drawing that power out in its entirety, wouldn't *you* want to know how it worked on the inside?"

He...can't mean...

He'd read the reports.

He knew of the unknown supernatural power possessed by a boy in Academy City.

And his right arm, said to nullify any holiness or sorcery.

"I could use it." Fiamma smiled, holding his right arm straight out. His third arm, which had broken apart, moved as well, under its own power, as if in response. "With this, God's "Likeness," the power of Michael, I *will* handle it perfectly. And for that, preparations are necessary."

Of course, just having the requisite materials didn't mean you could control a spell. In order to suppress an overwhelming power, you needed overwhelming knowledge beyond the realm of man. And the Roman pope knew of such a treasure trove of knowledge. The singular crystallization of knowledge, with all the world's grimoires collected in one place.

Fiamma must have known what the pope was thinking from his

expression. His smile widened. "The Index of Prohibited Books. Those Brits really put together something fantastic."

And that was why…

…he needed England.

Not the person herself, who was staying in Academy City for now—but specifically Great Britain.

"I won't…let you," muttered the pope.

He dragged his blood-covered body to its feet. He thought that if he asked for guidance from God's Right Seat, if he became one of them and aimed for the *kami-jou*, he could save many more of his followers. He hadn't wanted such a thing to elevate his own position and power as the pope. He hadn't become the pope to create a world where innocent lambs were used as stepping stones.

That was why the man now stood in the way.

The futures of two billion were behind him.

"This will be fun."

Fiamma laughed, his giant arm still level with the ground.

"One-sided contests are ridiculous but still fun."

Ga-boom!!

They didn't even clash.

Fiamma's overwhelming power simply pierced the pope, sending him flying.

St. Peter's Square was destroyed into fine particles. The explosion's aftermath knocked over several buildings and caused the already-damaged basilica to collapse even further. Part of the outer wall encircling Vatican City fell. That was where the pope had been blown to.

The commotion made the Vatican's guard, who were convinced there could never be a crisis in a place like this, finally come running. At first, they stared at Fiamma with a blank look. They probably didn't think a mere person could cause destruction on this scale. Eventually, a few snapped out of it to do their duty. They were crushed and sent flying. And that was when the "dominator" was sure of that power's destruction.

"Hmm?" he muttered, looking at the Vatican's outer wall, thoroughly destroyed.

Strange. No victims.

By all rights, the aftermath from his previous strike should have turned Rome, outside the wall, into a mountain of rubble hundreds of meters across. But the destruction was actually only inside the Vatican. It hadn't reached the city outside.

"He took it all himself? What a guy."

Fiamma hummed to himself, heading for the mostly destroyed St. Peter's Basilica.

Neither a lowly guard nor heavyweights like archbishops or cardinals could say a word.

The blood-soaked Roman pope collapsed against the outside wall of a house.

Fiamma hadn't bothered to conceal the explosion. Now there was a huge disturbance in the area, with people thinking it was a terrorist bombing.

An ambulance siren wailed somewhere.

He thought for a moment that there had been casualties, but apparently, it was coming closer in order to carry *him*.

He looked around, but none of the houses looked caved in.

Several windows had broken due to the shattered fragments of the outer wall, but it didn't look like anyone had died.

It put a faint smile on his lips, when suddenly, he noticed a girl in filthy clothes looking at him from a small alley between houses.

It was dangerous here.

He tried to tell her, but he couldn't put together real words.

The girl was shouting something at him, maybe to keep him from losing consciousness. She wasn't carrying any bandages or disinfectant. However, the pope, who didn't desire any more technology than necessary, was actually thankful for it. After his brush with a massive evil, this little act of kindness touched his heart.

"Hah. Now there's something."

He heard a voice.

He looked up and saw a woman wrapped in yellow clothing standing there.

Vento of the Front.

"Damaging your honor to save the lost lambs and, in the meantime, thinking about a nobody worrying about you? And you still hate being chosen by others? You *were* elected to this position, Mr. Pope."

"...Britain."

The pope's mouth managed to open between gasps of breath.

He spoke, though it was mostly blood coming out.

"Fiamma's target...is in...Britain..."

"Nobody gives me orders," spat Vento. "But I'll let it slide this time, since we both want to kill that shithead."

Vento fell silent for a moment. The filthy girl was glaring at Vento in challenge.

"Such good malice," she said, smiling thinly. "And you're in luck. If I had my actual weapon, you'd be dead where you stand."

The ambulance siren approached.

Vento said nothing more before disappearing into an alley between houses—seeming more familiar with it than the filthy girl.

Little Venice, London.

The archbishop of the English Puritan Church, its highest authority, Laura Stuart, lay on a boat, napping. The boat was on a man-made river controlled by several gates. As the name Venice might imply, they seemed to be going for some of the Venetian feel... but they'd messed something up, and though the sight was beautiful, it was wholly unlike that city. It wasn't even a city on the water or anything. This was simply a dock where three rivers met.

Behind the scenes, this was also a place meant to reproduce and allude to the geography of Venice, the city constructed atop the sea, from a magical viewpoint. Very few people knew the truth, though.

"I would have at least preferred a rowboat..."

Laura cast a bored glance to the boat's rear. There was a man there, who must have been the captain, but the boat had a small engine on it.

"A report, ma'am."

The captain had come to her with work. She'd finally slipped out of St. George's Cathedral, and now this man was ruining the atmosphere. Laura frowned but prompted him to continue.

"We have evidence of internal strife in the Roman Orthodox Church. The pope appears to have been involved. We don't know if he's alive. We've confirmed they transported him to a hospital, but the situation is unpredictable."

"..."

He mixed in speculatory information based on eyewitness reports from Rome and mana flows, detailing this alleged "internal strife."

"Judging from the massive quantity of mana we observed inside the Vatican, the damages should have swelled to many times what it did...Please give our calculations a bit more time, ma'am. We may have been mistaken somewhere."

"Hmph. You shan't find anything. An entire city is at His Holiness's back. The result is clearer than looking at a fire."

She turned, her expression now hidden from the captain. As she did, she muttered the words, "Damned good person."

The captain couldn't determine how much those words meant, or what she felt when she said them. Laura Stuart's age was not what it appeared to be, and the experience she'd accrued was an order of magnitude removed from regular people. That was why the captain couldn't understand what she was thinking.

"...But I'm sure you were smiling, you damned good person."

However, the entirely average captain got one impression.

Somehow, in some way, Laura Stuart sounded lonely.

A windowless building stood at a corner of Academy City.

This building boasted enough defenses to survive a nuclear blast, but it had been designed for a single person.

The Academy City General Board chairperson, Aleister.

On the lips of that "person" floating upside-down in a giant glass tube was a smile.

He was watching a square window displayed directly in the air.

Information from the Underline.

The Underline was a unique network made up of incredibly small machines scattered throughout the city.

Normally, this window would display any information he wanted. Now, all he saw was gray noise. Because of the major explosion that occurred after defeating Acqua of the Back, the Underline information network was temporarily disabled. It was made with extremely unusual technology, but the pieces were just seventy nanometers in size. Sometimes explosive blasts and shock waves damaged them.

The noise occurring in one area had spread to other spots in the network, causing an overload on the entire thing. It would be a few hours before it was completely restored. For Aleister, it was like someone had removed an arm, but he merely smiled.

"As I thought, I will have to do something about this problem. It must be rectified..."

In fact, he seemed happy—as though it was clear to him now what he needed to do.

The swarm of machines surrounding Aleister did a multilateral analysis of the information from right before the Underline had gone down, unifying all the noise-covered fragments into clearer, effective intelligence. Vivid colors appeared on the gray screen, immediately converting to a crucial report on display.

The report regarded the power a certain boy's right arm possessed.

Various chemical equations danced, calculating his brain's activity from the quantities of oxygen he inhaled and the carbon dioxide he exhaled. From the counterbalancing of the AIM diffusion fields prevalent in Academy City, they calculated his right hand's power and characteristics.

From start to finish, this was a world constructed of only science.

Aleister scanned the letters in the corner of the monitor, his smile deepening.

Before this "person," who appeared to be both adult and child, both man and woman, both saint and sinner, was the following report:

Illogical phenomenon-rejecting Point Central O maintaining stability level 3.

Specified core speed confirmed, now idling at center.

Plan influence coefficient for specimen named Imagine Breaker: 98%.

Strength as main plan backbone, along with Academy City no. 1, operating according to plan.

AFTERWORD

For those of you who have been following the series one novel at a time, it's good to see you again.

For those who have pulled off the incredible feat of reading seventeen volumes at once, it's a pleasure to meet you.

I'm Kazuma Kamachi.

This afterword section will reach its twentieth anniversary soon. I should be used to it by now, but it feels very much as inept and awkward as the main story sometimes.

The theme of this volume was "chosen ones." The occult keyword was *saint*. Acqua's spell is made up of things like the Adoration of Mary, but the basic foundation here was the clash between saints.

The Saintbreaker used by Itsuwa (or rather, all of Amakusa), as you might realize by reading back over Volume 9, is a monumental task. I'd like you to consider the power balance of Amakusa on the magic side ruined now that they've revealed a major trick up their sleeves. (Of course, Tatemiya got to show off his own tactical prowess, pleading with their Priestess to return as their leader, lest their situation grow worse.)

A few pieces of information relating to the core of the series itself showed up here and there in this book. You might find it interesting to try going over all the information you've been given so far. What information was revealed at what points, and when was that information subverted? If you investigate, you might be able to catch a glimpse of what might happen in the series from here on out.

I'd like to thank my editor, Mr. Miki, and my illustrator, Mr. Haimura. The book was filled with a lot of surprisingly onerous battle sequences, which I'm sorry about. Thank you for sticking with me.

And thanks to all my readers as well. The hidden parts of this series are somehow the only parts that are in a huge jumble, which I apologize for, but thank you very much for following along thus far.

Now then, as I close the pages on this book,
and as I pray you'll open the next pages safely,
today, at this hour, I lay down my pen.

Seems like even Itsuwa is becoming a not-so-normal girl now.

Kazuma Kamachi

YEAAAAHHHH
Excitement
Volume 16 & Anime Adaptation
CONGRATULATIONS.
... Might be nice.
Salutations!
I apologize for the eye poison again. I'm Kogino, artist for the comic adaptation in Gangan. Index is finally getting an anime adaptation of its very own. And when I think of it being an anime...
I think of Himegami!!
I started getting flustered when she was looking so carefully at the night parade pamphlet in Volume 10...
I can't get enough of that pitiful-type moe!!
...It's a shame she probably won't have much of a chance to appear in the manga...

Congratulations
on Volume 16's release
and the anime adaptation
I'm here again, getting carried away after Volume 14. I can't wait to see Touma, Index, and the others animated.
冬川基
Motoi Fuyukawa